Memorial Day

Bryan Serwatka

First published in the United Kingdom by Bryan Serwatka 2012

Copyright © Bryan Serwatka 2012

ISBN 9781475152982

For Dom

A wild chorus of young voices counts down from **ten**. Their thundering synchronized chant fills the halls of Bell High School. **Nine**. The students are out of their chairs, poised by the doors with their bags slung over their shoulders. **Eight**. Loose papers, empty ballpoint pens, and the skeletons of spiral notebooks lie discarded throughout the corridors. **Seven**. A clutter of poster-boards held up by sticky blue putty line the walls of Tom Woodbine's literature classroom. His whiteboard is littered with an explosion of his students' graffitied autographs and slogans of well-wishes. **Six**. A dusty MDF bookshelf in the back corner of the room stands surrounded by white cardboard boxes and plastic chairs stacked dangerously high. **Five**. A tinny snippet of a pop song plays through a mobile phone underneath the cacophony. **Four**. A group of girls huddled by the door hug each other tightly with tears in their eyes. **Three**. Tom sits at his desk and a smile uninvitedly sneaks its way out the left side of his mouth. **Two**. The floors shake with the low, sub-bass buzz of foot-stomping and applause rippling through the building. **One**. Shouting, laughing and smiling, brimming with an energy never displayed within the classrooms, the students burst forth into the blinding summer sun.

The ring of the bell went unnoticed, drowned out by the triumphant fanfare of the vacation now at hand. Though there would be no students waiting to speak to Tom after class, he waited for the halls to empty before daring to leave the classroom. He watched from his chair as the students flooded the hallways, surging towards the exits. Tom heard three tiny knocks on his open classroom door and saw a slender hispanic girl with straight black hair to her shoulders standing at the threshold. Susan Ortega calmly smiled, grasping the padded shoulder straps of her rucksack as the hissing chaos of the crowd worked its way around her. The haste and projected significance of the day seemed lost to them both if only for a brief moment. Susan nodded and waved to Tom before she cast herself back into the impetuous rush of the mob.

Silence slowly worked its way through the halls as Tom gathered the last few papers and trinkets from his desk and placed them in a large white cardboard box. With the rest of the faculty either celebrating in the cafeteria or sweating on crowd-control duty outside, Tom walked the empty littered hallways to the office, imagining the passages as streets and alleys in a dusty ghost-town with tumbleweeds ambling past. Tom silently waved as he passed the vacant front desk then left the building with the box on his shoulder and a skip in his step. He drove along the expressway with the windows down, placidly passing the limitless chain restaurants, car lots, and mini-malls. His blue and white striped shirt darkened on his chest and under his arms in the heat and humidity of the early Texas summer. Reports of protests, economic crisis, celebrity bilge, and the now-negative presidential electioneering flooded in through the car radio - but none of it could illicit a response from Tom.

Awkwardly carrying the box, his bag, and a thick stack of mail he fetched from his mailbox outside, Tom clambered through the front door of his apartment. Flat-pack bookshelves heaving with Tom's worn literary collection lined the walls of his living room with small framed prints and family photos dotting the few spaces between. Tom placed the box on his countertop then walked to his stereo and pressed shuffle. A short Schnittke string quartet track started as he rustled through the wad of bills, delivery menus, a University of Texas alumni newsletter, and his voter registration renewal. Tom then compulsively sat down on his sofa with his tablet computer and began his daily post-work browsing of email, social networking sites, and internet news.

Looking out to the rest of the world while surrounded by the creature comforts of home seemed to have a centering effect for him. As the stereo shuffled to an ambient electronic song by Mogwai, Tom slowly slid to lie down on the sofa with the computer resting flat on his stomach. The intense May sun streamed in through the thin bamboo mini-blinds and sharply sliced Tom's living room with hundreds of thin horizontal lines, reminding him of the screen of an old interlaced cathode-ray television.

Tom expected a call that evening from his older sister Samantha. Sam had two kids, five-year-old Brandon and two-year-old Shelley, and had left her husband the previous summer for another man - also named Tom. Having to juggle two Toms in their lives terrible confused the children until Sam insisted they would now be calling their uncle 'Uncle Tom'. Tom tried to explain the literary meaning of the term 'Uncle Tom' to Sam and her new beau, but Sam didn't get the joke, the new Tom didn't care, and the kids couldn't possibly understand it for at least another ten years or so.

With his shoes still on his feet, Tom began to drift asleep as the familiar ethereal hum of the third movement of John Adams' *Harmonium* slowly began to fill the room. Tense strings and horns patiently built for minutes before the chorus burst into a full roar , shrieking the words of Emily Dickinson's 'Wild Nights'. Tom stirred awake. Though he had listened to this record countless times, it always precipitated goosebumps and shivers. In his considered life of structure and routine, Tom treasured anything that could rouse such a physical response. As the music boiled his blood, a hunger in his belly made him feel slightly faint - and like a sobering slap in the face, Tom's phone loudly rang on the countertop next to the box.

The phone's screen shone the smiling, tanned face of David

Matthews. David only called once or twice a month - usually on a weekday evening. Unsure whether he wanted to answer or not, Tom let the phone ring three times before giving in.

"Hey Dave."

"Hey Tom," David purred.

"What's up?"

"Can I come over tonight?"

Gone are the days of pleasantries, Tom thought. He sighed and said, "Dave, it's been a long day - last day of the school year. I don't know if I'm up for entertaining."

"Don't worry, I'll do all the entertaining."

And gone are the subtleties. "What time were you thinking?"

"I dunno, maybe nine?"

"Could you make it eight? I've got loads of work in the morning."

"Sure thing, Tom. See you at eight."

Tom has always found David painfully casual. Tom knew that David worked in a hospital, but he didn't know much more than that - nor did he particularly want to know. Details only tend to complicate things in a relationship like theirs.

Two years ago, Tom and David met head-to-head in the semifinals of a local charity tennis tournament. Tom had played tennis at a competitive level since he was a teenager, but he could never break into the top tiers. He lacked the killer instinct essential for serious tennis and tended to get lost in the repetitive mantra of the rallies without ever really focusing on actually defeating his opponents. David had only been playing tennis a short while before entering the tournament, but he was a natural athlete with an intuition and grace that made his every move an effortless work of art. Tom found that watching David play tennis - or do anything for that matter - was mesmerizing. David dominated the contest, running Tom from sideline to sideline until he was dead on his feet. At the end of the short match, they walked up to the center of the net to shake hands. David was kind and jovial, looking as if he had barely even warmed up. Tom, however, dripped with sweat and could barely manage light conversation before he slumped off to the side bench. As he pulled his drenched shirt over his head, frustrated and exhausted, Tom looked over to see David watching him like a hawk. David's eyes looked more focused and predatory there on the sidelines than they did on court. Still totally perplexed, Tom watched David slowly walk towards his bench as if viewing a mirage slowly appear.

"It's 'Tom', isn't it?"

Tom dozily nodded.

"Would you like to have a drink with me some time?"

"Yeah I guess so. When?"

"How about tonight?"

"Don't you have another match?"

David beamed as he said, "Yeah but it'll be a piece of cake - I'll be done by seven. How about the Japanese place at eight?"

"Can we make it nine? I have to drop by my sister's tonight."

"Then I'll see you there at nine."

Another effortless victory for Mr. Matthews, Tom thought.

The local sushi bar was the only bar in the area whose walls weren't lined with televisions perpetually tuned to loud sports channels with even louder patrons screaming at the screens. Over a pair of Japanese lagers, Tom and David chatted about the tournament.

"Look Tom" David coolly said, "there's something different about you, and we both know what that is."

Bewildered, Tom said, "Sorry, but I really don't follow."

"You saw me checking you out on the court and you didn't bat an eye. Then when I asked you out for a drink, you didn't hesitate."

Tom laughed and said, "Ah. That kind of different."

"Why don't we head back to mine for some more drinks? I do like this place, but I'm sick of paying eight bucks a beer."

Beer was the last thing on David's mind. As the front door at David's apartment shut behind them, David grabbed Tom by the hips and pushed him firmly to the wall. David pushed his groin into Tom's and, with his lips, he slowly traced Tom's neck from his collarbone to the back of his ear.

"I want to taste that smooth chest of yours," David said breathing heavily. "It's the only thing I've been able to think about all night."

Since that evening, the two of them have regularly met to 'unwind' - as they called it - even though Tom could never see even a glimpse of tension in David that could ever possibly need unwinding. Still, he never complained.

After a quick meal of pasta with olive oil and parmesan, Tom opened a beer and flicked through some photos on his computer. In his inbox was a message notification from a gay dating website. These sites were mostly anonymous hookup mediums for the impatiently horny and always left Tom feeling glum. To him they seemed like a platform gay men used to create a persona based not on how they view themselves, but how they believe others want to see them. After the first few meetings, Tom noticed that there tended to be a disconnect between a person and their profile, and from then on he started trying to guess what the deviation would be prior to the rendezvous. In no time, the predictably depressing results of Tom's guessing game became more than enough of a reason for him to stay away from these sites.

Having some time to kill, Tom opened the message and saw a thumbnail image of a man in black sunglasses laughing while pinning his windblown sombrero to his head.

Well that's a start - at least he's wearing clothes.

The message read: 'Hi there! I'm Mike and I've just moved up to Belton from Houston. I'm trying to make some friends in the area and came across your profile. I'm a total bookworm like you, and any fan of Kate Bush and Talking Heads is already a friend of mine! Anyway if you're free some time I'd really love to meet up over coffee and pick your brain about the area. - Mike :)'

Seems innocent enough, Tom thought.

Tom's phone rang on the coffee table in front of the sofa - it was Sam. Tom's mind was elsewhere and he didn't want to speak to her so he let it ring. She sent a text message seconds later:

'Having friends over Sat at 2. Kids would like to see you. Mom might come. Sx'

Yeah right - like Mom's coming up for snacks.

A few years back, just after Sam's first wedding, Tom's parents bought a house on Galveston Island only eight blocks away from the beach. The Woodbines always met as a family at Christmas and occasionally Easter, but since their move, Tom rarely saw or spoke to his parents.

Tom shut off his computer and walked to the kitchen. He slid the large cardboard box on the countertop towards him and carefully cut the brown packing tape with a paring knife. He removed several handfuls of styrofoam pellets before reaching into the box for a short chain made of metal wire hearts and stars. As it jingled in his hands, Tom experienced a sense of calm that cut right through the already sedate atmosphere of the evening.

At 7:48, a light knock sounded on Tom's door.

He's early.

Once David learned the numerical code to the complex gate there was never any announcement to his arrival. Tom had tidied the apartment earlier, anticipating David's eagerness, and left an Andrew Bird album playing in the background. Tom opened the door to see David stood facing the opposite direction as he watched the sun dip below the tree-line across the parking lot. The silhouettes of tiny oak leaves swayed in front of the sun, now magenta and double its size near the horizon making the oak trees seem simultaneously beautiful and insignificant. Tom stared at David's back and shoulders, admiring his profile. In that perfect light, anyone standing in front of Tom's door would have looked glamorous. But just for good measure, David managed to look absolutely divine.

"Hey Dave, what are you looking at?"

"Nothing really. It's just a lovely evening," David said, slowly turning to face Tom. "Still, I'd be lying if I said I thought we'd be wasting this sunset by staying indoors."

"Do come in."

Tom shut the door behind David and, as expected, David pushed him to the wall to kiss him. Even David's kisses had a style and finesse that was totally his own: soft but intense, just a little tongue, and always ending with a playfully light bite on Tom's lower lip. David untucked Tom's shirt from his slacks and worked his hands underneath to his hipbones then up to caress the curves of his shoulder blades. When Tom realized the blinds were still open, he grabbed David's hand and dragged him to the bedroom, shutting off the stereo on route. They undressed each other at the foot of Tom's bed. Each knew his partner's body well enough to adeptly maneuver about, summoning reactions at will. Each knew the other's wants and limits; never did they breach the unsaid boundaries of undesired discomfort. Each got exactly the amount of physical human contact and release he needed without the attachment he didn't.

At 9:36, they took turns showering. In the steam-choked bathroom they behaved with an etiquette reminiscent of a locker room with their eyes never wandering below the collarbone. Both men moved with a slow, drained litheness as they hung up the towels, put on short white robes, and moved into the now-dark living room. Tom turned on the light and trotted ahead to close the blinds as David reclined on the sofa. David switched on the television and they silently, intently watched clips from an overseas tennis tournament. David occasionally let out a subdued whoop or clapped his hands at a great rally but nothing was said between them. By ten o'clock, David was back at Tom's front door, fully dressed and ready to leave.

"Until next time," he said before kissing Tom on the cheek and walking out the door.

Tom nodded and watched as David sauntered down the corridor to his car, looking out to the trees where the sun set earlier. Tom's neighbors Lily and Steven sat in deck chairs on the opposite side of the parking lot, enjoying a smoke in the last warm hours of the day. As their gazes moved from David back to Tom's apartment, Tom quickly shut the front door and walked to the kitchen to fetch a beer. He then went to the living room and switched on the local news to watch a woman with teased hair announce a trailer park fire that killed nine people. As Bob from sports came on the screen, Tom's phone flashed with another text message from Sam:

'Just wanted to let you know that Mom is now staying at mine for the weekend. Sx'

Great.

Tom stared at the sofa that had just held David's clean, warm body, mentally tracing his imprint. Feeling a bit glum after one of David's visits wasn't uncommon for Tom, but something about this last encounter left him feeling totally despondent. Like it or not, his regular, unromantic flings with David were the closest thing Tom ever had to romance. There had never been anyone in his life for whom he actually felt some true personal connection. Petrified by the thought, he switched off the television and sat in silence.

'Anyway - if you're free some time I'd really love to meet up over coffee and pick your brain about the area. - Mike :) '

Tom remembered the emotive message from the dating site and reached for his computer. As he quickly skimmed through Mike's profile, Tom immediately noticed that Mike seemed very happy in every single picture. Of course, people generally don't portray themselves as anything but happy, but in all of these pictures Mike seemed genuinely, ecstatically happy - which made Tom slightly jealous. Tom tapped a text message on his phone's screen:

'Hi Mike, Tom from _____.com here. I'm pretty much free for the next couple of weeks if you'd like to meet.'

2

Tom's last beer woke him up at 2:13 AM. As he left the bathroom, he slipped into the robe David wore earlier and walked to the living room, automatically checking his phone for messages. One from Mike had come only minutes after his last text:

'Hi Tom! I haven't found work yet so I've got nothing but free time. How does tomorrow at 4 sound? Mike x'

Tom replied, 'I'll be at work until at least 4:30 - can we do 5?'

Just as Tom set his phone back down on the charger, it began to vibrate. He didn't hesitate to answer. He yawned loudly and said, "Hi, is this Mike?"

"It is, yeah. Sorry - you sound really tired."

"No, it's alright" Tom said while unsuccessfully trying to stifle another yawn. "So Mike, what moved you here from Houston?"

"Uh well, basically, I got divorced and wanted to start fresh somewhere else. There's obviously more to it but the details would send you to sleep in no time, especially at this hour. I moved in a few days ago and have been spending all my time sorting out the new house formalities and trying to unpack. I didn't realize I had so much junk so I've been selling loads of it online. This evening I took over two hundred photos of all my old junk. ... Sorry, I'm rambling."

"No, it's okay." Tom realized that this was the first actual conversation he'd had since work.

"Where do you think we should meet?"

"There's a nice little coffee shop just outside the main gates of the university building. Do you know the area?"

"Not very well, but I know where the coffee shop is. I live just around the corner."

"Nice neighborhood. Anyway, tomorrow's my last day of work for a couple of months. I'm a teacher and I'm only really there tomorrow to tidy my classroom, sit through a few dull meetings, and sign off on some forms."

"Would you rather go for a celebratory drink instead?"

Tom laughed and said, "We'll see. After the departmental meetings I may need one. I can handle students but I find teachers to be really hard work."

"Well I'm up for either. You've got my number - feel free to call when you'd like."

"Thanks Mike. See you tomorrow."

"Sweet dreams Tom."

Tom didn't dream that night - at least he couldn't remember dreaming - but he did wake and get out of bed with ease. The humdrum, detached hesitation he normally felt before leaving for work had been overtaken by a sense of composure. He drove into the school parking lot at the usual time finding it much emptier than he expected. Many of his workmates had gone out the night before to celebrate and would slowly trickle in with collectively sore heads. If there was any one day a teacher could show up late to work, today was that day. When Tom said he found teachers to be hard work, he genuinely meant it. Most of the teachers he worked with were cliquish and constantly condescending towards those around them. When Tom socialized with them outside of school in bars and restaurants, they were very demanding of the staff, constantly patronizing them and always finding an arbitrary reason for not leaving any gratuity. However, there were two fellow teachers at his school that Tom considered as friends.

Kate was a few years older than Tom and had been teaching history for over a decade now. Her husband, fifteen years her senior, was a military officer when they first married, and over their years together they constantly moved from one base to another before finally settling in Central Texas. Kate's husband voluntarily retired six years ago at the passing of the Military Commissions Act of 2006 and had spent the past few months working tax-free in Afghanistan as a contractor alongside the military reconstruction. Since his stint overseas began, Tom and Kate saw each other almost weekly for drinks and a film. They usually sought out film adaptations of books to nitpick the flaws then inevitably decide that the book was better. Their last meeting was particularly boozy.

"You know, it's like a fucking jail sentence for me. I only cheated on him when we were stationed in Okinawa because he wasn't around much - but now he's not here at all! I don't think I have the energy to have another affair, but there are times when I just crave a man's touch. You know what that's like right? Oh who am I kidding! You of all people must know exactly what that's like! How's that David guy you've been seeing?"

"I don't really *see* him. It's just a physical thing."

"You lucky little shit."

Another teacher Tom occasionally met outside work was Jeremy, the head of the school's music department. Jeremy was a portly gent in his mid-50s with a scraggly red and grey beard and a penchant for trying to bed women half his age. Both Jeremy and Tom were self-proclaimed 'foodies' and liked to meet at fledgling restaurants to bitch about work and discreetly compare the eateries to their cross-town equivalents. Tom always found it amusing that his meetings with both teachers typically ended up in some form of critical assessment of the outing itself - yet it never jaded his enthusiasm for their company. A year or so ago, over Singha beer and large bowls of steaming pad thai, Jeremy admitted that while he attended university, he slept with one of his fellow male students to 'experiment'. Jeremy confessed that after fifteen minutes of tense fumbling and teeth-clicking kisses, he found himself unaroused and apologized to the guy before sending him on his way.

In a part of the world that stays warm eight months of the year, summer as a concept is hard to comprehend, but through sheer anticipation, teachers are those most attuned to the slow, systematic changes of their local environments as summer approaches. They know the distinct smell of grass scorched by mid-day watering, the gradual snow-blind brightening of sunlight reflected off the sidewalks, and the dust lines on buildings formed from the fine grit swirled by mid-May gusts. As the world around him prepared for summer, Tom normally focused on his lesson plans for the remedial summer school sessions for students who didn't earn passing marks - but this year was different. In January, as Tom read Frost's 'The Road Not Taken' aloud to his students, he felt a growing sense of self-reproach as the passion of the prose felt alien to him. Afterwards he tried to explain the poem and make it seem relevant to his students - and to himself - but he was left feeling like a fraud stood at the front of the class. In an instant, the reliable comfort of Tom's untroubled life felt like a consolation prize for complacent idleness. Then and there, he decided some change had to be made. With the summer off, Tom set aside a couple thousand dollars and planned to show up at the airport with his bags packed, passport in hand, and take the most unusual deal the airlines could offer. He would find accommodation in the most populous area and stay out all night every night to take in the local vibes. However, as the hectic final weeks of exams consumed Tom's mind, he began to forget the feeling of unease that sparked this mental streak of adventure and his fantasy slowly faded.

Over the past week, Tom slowly cleared his classroom of textbooks and decorative ephemera between and after classes to ease the summer transition. As Tom entered his classroom, he instinctively shut his eyes while switching on the lights to avoid the disorienting reflection off the glossy, windowless concrete walls. He turned to see his whiteboard empty; his students' scrawls obviously cleaned in his absence. Sweeping the perimeter of the room, Tom began clearing the walls of poster-boards, fire escape routes, and other papers. He paused halfway as he removed a charcoal facsimile of Blake's *The Tyger* - one of Susan's works. Susan was one of the brightest and most well-spoken and outgoing students Tom ever had the privilege to teach. She always worked on her own and, unlike her peers, dependably read the assigned reading and was prepared for class discussions. Sadly, at the beginning of this past school year, Susan's mother was killed in a widely publicized incident that briefly captured the attention of the nation. Understandably, Susan was deeply shaken by her mother's death, but her friends and teachers noticed that she stopped being the friendly, talkative, warm girl they all knew. As time went on, those around her even began to forget what Susan's voice sounded like. Because she passed all her exit exams and kept a solid grade point average, the school administration wasn't too concerned. They saw her graduation itself as a success and patted each other on the backs for a job well done. Nevertheless, Tom watched Susan's transition closely and knew firsthand that something else continued to fuel this girl's transformation.

3

Both of Susan's parents worked for the Bell County Sheriff's Department. Her father's ex-military experience helped him advance up the ranks of the administrative department while her mother worked as a deputy investigator. On September 4, 2011, Mrs. Ortega and her partner were dispatched to investigate a report of violent domestic disturbance in a remote part of the county. The husband involved was accused of pushing his wife into a bathtub causing heavy bruising to her face, back, and legs. Officer Ortega wrote down the wife's story while her partner talked to the husband in another room. The woman broke down in tears as she showed Officer Ortega several older scars and bruises that covered her groin and thighs. Ortega only left the room for a few seconds to have a word with her partner, but moments later the wife entered the room with a pistol in her hands, sobbing uncontrollably as the officers tried to calm her down. With her hands in the air, Ortega told the woman she needed to put the gun down if she wanted her abusive husband to pay for his abuse. As the sobbing woman lowered the gun, her husband reached for Ortega's gun still in its holster. In a moment of pure reaction, the wife fired four shots. The first bullet hit her husband in his abdomen, the next lodged into the wall behind them, and the others hit Ortega in the chest and neck.

It took the paramedics fifteen minutes to reach Officer Ortega and another fifteen back to the emergency room. Susan's family lived near the hospital and were able to arrive just as the two ambulances drove under the covered parking bay. Susan watched from behind the ambulance as the driver and her mother's partner spilled out from the front and ran to open the back doors. Inside a female paramedic, drenched in sweat and blood, stood poised to lower Mrs. Ortega's gurney. Susan vividly remembered the paramedic's light brown hair tied back in a knot, the few freckles that lightly dotted her cheekbones, and her bright green eyes filled with focus and determination. Susan fell to her knees as the ambulance crew rushed her mother in through the ER's sliding doors. Her father José followed closely behind while carrying her two-year-old brother Roberto. Though the rest of her memory of the event is blurry, Susan would forever remember the feathery sight of ambulance lights erratically flickering through her tears and the sensation of knobbly asphalt digging into her bare knees, the hard tarmac still warm from the sun's rays.

The paramedic stepped outside moments later to see Susan in the middle of the parking lot, her stare still fixed on the ambulance. As she neared Susan, the paramedic looked down at her blood-soaked hands and jacket and took off her outer uniform and wiped her hands on it. The closer she got to Susan, the more distraught she felt, and as she dropped to her hands and knees in front of Susan, she began to weep. The peculiar sound of the sobbing paramedic broke Susan's transfixion and, without a thought, Susan put her arms around the woman.

"I'm sorry, I'm sorry - oh my God I'm so sorry!" the woman cried.

"I know. It's OK."

Susan picked pebbles from her knees as she stood, holding her hand out to the paramedic. As they walked hand-in-hand past the parked ambulance, its floor coated in blood, the paramedic said to Susan, "You don't want to look at that," but nothing could break the young girl's expressionless gaze. They walked through the ER lobby and down a series of hallways to a row of plush maroon chairs where José sat surrounded by doctors and his wife's partner. Little Roberto played with a nurse in an empty room, oblivious to the turmoil around him.

The paramedic put her hand on Mr. Ortega's trembling shoulder and said, "I found her outside in the parking lot."

"Susan... Your mother -"

"I know Dad."

José let out a violent, choking cough then sobbed into his hands. Susan reached down to embrace her father, but he threw his hands in the air as he quickly rose, nearly knocking Susan over.

"Couldn't you have done anything else?!" He stood face-to-face with the paramedic, pushing his pointed finger into her cheek. "Couldn't you have done your fucking job?! Maybe if you did, my kids would still have their mother! If you were a man I -"

Susan spun her father around by his shoulder and struck him across the face with a slap that echoed down the glass walls and linoleum floors. Speechless, he fell back into his seat while his daughter stared down at him with shame.

José didn't speak a word until the morning of his wife's funeral. After helping Roberto dress for the memorial service, José walked into the living room where his daughter sat watching cartoons. José couldn't look her in the eyes as he talked.

"Susan, you were right to hit me. I shouldn't have spoken to the paramedic that way. I know this might sound crazy, but as you slapped me, I looked up at you and saw you as your mother. It was as if it was her hand that hit me and her face that looked down at me with shame."

Friends, family, acquaintances, councilmen, police officers, and even the local congressman attended the funeral, filling the small chapel far over capacity. Dozens of photographers and reporters both local and national waited outside for the bereaved.

The Ortegas sat at the front of the church after the service as floods of people in floods of tears walked past with words of sympathy. The day before the funeral, Susan asked her father if she could be one of the pallbearers, but he vacantly never replied. As six men approached her mother's coffin to carry it to the hearse, Susan stood and pulled away her cousin Raoul - an all-state football plater - to take his place. Her father sat frozen to his chair.

Susan scanned the reactions of all those watching her as she walked down the aisle towards the doors. Stood in the shadows of a pillar in the far corner of the church was the paramedic. Susan recognized her immediately and gave a knowing, thankful smile that was identically returned. They stared into each others' eyes until Susan reached the door of the church where the photographers waited. Susan would always remember the deafening sound and blinding lights of the wall of cameras at the church's double doors. After a few seconds of their shimmering stuns, the cameras were lowered and all eyes were on Susan as her muscles shuddered and ached under the weight of the heavy white coffin. Three kilted bagpipers stood in front of the church blaring their droning tune as the coffin was carried towards the hearse. A well known national television reporter stood poised near the church gate ready to pounce with a microphone in hand and camera in tow, but as Susan passed him, his arms fell to his side and he couldn't speak. He lowered his head and tears coursed down his face sending a small landslide of muddy makeup down onto his lapel. One of the local newspaper photographers captured an early side-profile shot of Susan as she walked outside with the coffin held shoulder-height. The high-contrast, nearly black-and-white photo of her face was emblazoned by the horde of flashes so intense that the undoctored photograph had almost no color at all, giving the photo the feel of a century-old sepia portrait. The image was unavoidable for weeks and was used on the cover of several local, state, and national magazines. To this day, Susan has no recollection of any moment from spotting the paramedic to the second her mother's coffin started lowering into the earth. The death of Sharon Ortega and the face of her daughter were burned into the town's collective conscience and wouldn't be forgotten for generations.

4

As Tom cleared the walls of excess staples, blue putty, and bits of chewing gum - *the most contemptible substance on the planet* - a tiny CD player on a filing cabinet filled the classroom with the sounds of a post-rock album Tom knew by heart after hundreds of listens. Tom mentally associated the album with one of the first nights he and David spent together. The album played in Tom's living room, barely audible in the bedroom, but Tom noticed David's foot tapping along to the beat and David noticed Tom moving back and forth to the waltz. They both laughed deliriously and continued unwinding in rhythm.

With his sleeves rolled up and his shirt partly unbuttoned, Tom carried boxes full of books to the English storeroom at the far end of the South wing. After breaking a sweat, he began to curse himself for being lax on his exercise routine. On the fifth trek, Tom saw his friend Jeremy carrying two full garbage-bags and jogged to catch up with him. Jeremy looked drab as ever wearing an ancient faded tartan shirt and baggy grey trousers.

"Hey Jeremy - what have you got there?"

"Just some leftover decorations and books I borrowed to spruce up the music hall. You?"

"*Romeo and Juliet.*"

"Ah - young love and drug use. You can't really ask for more can you?"

"My students seemed to think so. You should have heard them groan when they found out I wasn't going to play the modern film in class. I'd say only ten to twenty percent of them actually read it."

Jeremy raised his hand and interrupted Tom saying, "Before

you start whining, I wanted to remind you that I leave for Australia on Tuesday. What do you say we try the new Italian place on 2nd Street some time before then? I've heard under good authority that the veal there is unbeatable."

"Sounds like a date Jeremy."

"Don't you wish!"

"Oh Jeremy," Tom sighed, "when will you give in to my wiles?"

"When you grow a pair of tits, shave that ridiculous 'designer' stubble, and stop acting so goddamn ladylike."

It's amazing how different teachers act when they know the students are away.

Kate looked shocked to see Tom and Jeremy as she rounded the corner. Her eyes narrowed as Jeremy purred, "Well hello Kate. You're looking stunning as usual."

Tom said, "Don't look so surprised Kate. You know what he's like."

"I remember the *Non-Denominational Holiday* party very well." At a staff Christmas party three years ago, Jeremy, drunk as ever, cornered Kate and said, "Merry Christmas Kate. Would you like to go to the library and let me finger through your catalog?" Kate was so stunned all she could do was laugh in his face. By the end of the night, rumor spread through the party and most of the staff had memorized his lecherous proposition verbatim.

"Kate darling, you and I both know our respective spouses were either out of the country on duty or at home blathering away to toy dogs, oblivious of her husband's needs and urges. All's fair in love and war, dear."

"You know, I really hoped you'd stay away after humiliating yourself."

"Well Kate, let's just say I can't *perform* these days without thinking about how low you made me feel. Honestly, it was the best thing to happen to me since I discovered mail-order Viagra and Craigslist."

"You really are disgusting!"

"That's it - now tell me I'm scum."

"Yuck," Kate said grimacing. "Tom, I was on my way to your classroom to ask you out for lunch today but I didn't expect Jeremy to be so far away from the girls' locker room."

"Isn't the head office catering this afternoon?" Tom asked.

"Yeah but you know what they're like. They'll have sandwiches laying uncovered on the buffet table for hours, oozing with room temperature, low-fat, mayo-like spread."

Jeremy said, "If we leave in the next 20 minutes we can catch the lunch specials at the River Bistro."

"I don't remember inviting you Jeremy. Besides, Tom and I have a bit of gossip to catch up on. You wouldn't want to hear about it anyway."

Tom gave Kate his his best puppy-eyed look. "Oh come on Kate. I'd really like to spend some time with the both of you before the break."

Kate never told Tom that this look of his did nothing but make her feel uncomfortable. "Fine, but only because I adore you Tom. Who's driving?"

Jeremy said, "I'd offer to drive but I've already had a couple drinks this morning."

Nobody seemed very surprised. They reconvened outside Kate's car a few minutes later. Both Kate and Tom had picked up on Jeremy's fusty odor of scotch, dog, and mothballs on the short drive to the bistro. They tried rolling down the windows and breathing through their mouths but the smell was pervasive.

Jeremy ordered a bottle of Chablis immediately as they were seated in the restaurant. As the waiter left, he asked, "So - what is this gossip you were going to catch up on?"

"There really isn't any gossip. Kate just wants me to talk about my sex life so she can fantasize about two naked men kissing and sweating together in a clean, child-free apartment. I highly doubt you want to hear any of it."

"Oh please. Just because it's not something we casually talk about doesn't mean that I'm not interested. I'm not one of these insecure guys who shuts off at the very mention of two men *or more* being together. I'm not that repressed."

Kate piped up, "So you don't mind hearing explicit details?"

Tom bashfully rose his hands in a peaceful gesture. "I'm glad that the two of you are so accepting but I don't really want to get into the minutiae of my private life."

"How's things with you and David?" Kate asked.

"So there's a *David* then!" Jeremy bellowed. "You never told me about a David! What's he like?"

"Listen, there isn't a *David*," Tom whispered. "He's just someone I occasionally have over for sex. There is absolutely nothing more to our relationship. Hell, there isn't even a relationship between the two of us. At times I feel no more than an erotic masseuse."

"Then why don't you see someone else?" Jeremy asked.

"You're not listening - I don't *see* him. I occasionally *see* other guys in the very same physical way."

The waiter arrived with Jeremy's wine and a shocked look on his face. Jeremy inspected the label then poured a small glass for Tom before filling his own. He lowered his voice and said, "Correct me if I'm wrong, Tom, but from what I've just heard I think you sound like you're rather lonely."

"I really don't know, Jeremy. Last night I sat at home after David left and was struck by the thought that there is no real passion or emotion in my life. I could feel that I wasn't feeling.

27

Now I know that sounds convoluted and pretty damn depressing, but it was one of the most clarifying moments of my life."

Kate sat back in her chair quietly observing the two men talk about feelings and tried to remember the last time she heard her husband mention anything on the topic.

Jeremy said, "I think you should at least try to put yourself out there and be open to whatever comes your way. The universe blesses those open to its influence."

"Wow Jeremy," Kate said, "I wouldn't have placed you as such a flower child. I agree totally, but I've gotta say, I didn't expect something like that to come out of your mouth. I'm surprised."

Jeremy leaned in to Kate. "You know Kate, there are other things I can do with my mouth that would surprise you."

The waiter appeared with a basket of bread and another shocked expression. The food arrived shortly afterwards and the silence of contentment briefly swept across the table.

Tom said, "I'm seeing someone tonight. Well, not *seeing* him but we're meeting up for a coffee. He's new to the area and wants to make some friends."

"How did you meet?" Kate asked.

"He sent me a message on one of the gay dating websites. What caught my attention was that the message was free of the usual 'cocks', 'fucks', or 'holes'."

An elderly lady at the nearest table coughed loudly. Tom shrank into his seat and tried to convince himself it was unrelated. Kate and Jeremy turned bright red. After a few seconds of forced, uncomfortable silence, Tom continued, "He seems like a really happy guy though. He's recently divorced which makes me a bit wary."

"How come?" Jeremy asked.

"Well it means he's probably pretty new to the whole gay thing. Usually when guys come out, they go a bit wild. When I came out, I practically slept with any guy that came along. I'm really lucky I didn't do anything that could have cost me my health or my life even."

With his mouth full Jeremy said, "Well you'll never know what the guy's like until you meet him. ... Oh for fuck's sake - these potatoes are cold and unseasoned! Why did we come here?"

Kate pointed her fork at him from across the table and said, "*You* suggested it, you old grouch! I'm beginning to think all that Viagra is turning your brain to mush!"

In one calm gulp, Jeremy finished the remaining two-thirds of his glass and said, "Kate, dear, I no longer mind if my mind turns to mush. If I look at my life, I find my mind has done little for me other than blur and question the tangible, sincere cravings of my body. It led me into teaching the techniques and theory of music to mostly indifferent students when my heart wanted to compose and perform it. It led me to marry my wife for convenience and leave the woman my body craved. And now, I'm at the stage of life where both my mind and body are beginning to fail me, and the only experiences that give me pleasure involve tending to that one specific part of me that's anything but mush."

Tom raised his glass to Jeremy while Kate harshly whispered, "Don't fucking encourage him!"

Triumphantly, Jeremy said, "Now if you'll excuse me, I've got to platonically tend to the aforementioned member. Kate, if you're going to say something about me when I go, please make sure it's nice and saucy." He stood and bowed to his friends as he wandered away.

Kate waited for Jeremy to walk out of sight and said, "Tom - I've been seeing someone."

"Really?!"

"I've only seen him a couple of times. It's purely sexual - well it is for me - and I've never felt better."

"You sure it's only sexual? I distinctly remember the trauma from the last time this happened. What's the guy like?"

"Young."

Tom threw his head backwards and sighed, "Oh jeez."

"I know, I know. I want to say all this before Dumbledore comes back... He's a former student of mine from a few years ago." Tom opened his mouth to speak but Kate cut him short. "He's twenty-one now and is home from college for a couple months before going back to do his Masters. We ran into each other at the liquor store and he recognized me right away. I had no idea who he was when he approached me but I didn't care - he's stunning. I can't give you his name because you probably had him in your class."

"Fair enough."

"He flirted with me in the wine section and I just flirted back without thinking. After we paid, he walked up to my car outside the and told me that he'd like to go out for a drink. I said something stupid like, 'We just bought some booze - why go out and pay more for it? Haven't you heard about the recession?!' His parents were away so we went back to his place. His confidence turned me on like nothing else has in the last decade. It got a bit weird though."

"How?"

"He told me his little sister just finished the 9th grade. She could likely be in my class next year. What should I do?"

"Facial reconstructive surgery comes to mind. Aside from that or moving to another state, I really have no clue."

"He wants to see me again tonight. Thing is, I really want to see him too."

"Won't it be difficult with your kids at home all the time for the summer break? Where would you two go?"

"I've not really thought it all through. With all the bullshit formalities at work and sorting out childcare, I've been too busy to actually plan anything."

Jeremy entered the main dining room from a side hallway that led to the bathrooms. He walked towards the table.

Kate said, "Anyway I'd like to have a chat with you some time and finish this conversation without Jeremy around."

"Just call me whenever."

She blew a kiss to Tom and said, "Thanks gorgeous."

Jeremy threw himself into his chair. "What did I miss? What did she say about me?"

After Jeremy finished off the rest of the wine and generously paid the bill, they all headed back to work and valiantly fought through drowsiness during the staff seminars. Several teachers were still obviously hungover from the night before, but Jeremy sat amongst them fully intoxicated. Tom and Kate perched near an exit so they could be the first ones out of the auditorium. Kate spent her time text messaging her young lover and cunningly showing Tom the racy messages as they came in. Tom leaned back into his chair and felt a calm ease fall over him as he closed his eyes and daydreamed of his bare feet sinking into wet, warm sand.

5

At 5:10, Tom sat alone swirling a half-full mug of cold cappuccino and felt himself fidget. Mike had not yet shown up to the café and the caffeine boost wasn't helping Tom's nerves any. Mike finally jogged in at 5:14 looking a bit flush. He wore a blue t-shirt, khaki shorts, and a white Houston Astros baseball cap. A few strands of his wavy brown hair fell down onto his forehead underneath the brim of the cap. Tom had no problem recognizing Mike from his pictures and waved.

Mike walked over to Tom's table, breathing slightly heavily. "Hi Tom. It's nice to finally meet you."

"And you Mike."

Mike looked over his shoulders to see if anyone was listening. "It's actually *Andy* - I'm really sorry I lied and said my name was Mike. It's a bad habit of mine. Anyway I'm going to get a drink and be right back."

As Andy turned and walked to the counter, Tom grimaced. *This isn't a good start.*

Andy returned with an overpriced bottle of water and said, "Again I'm really sorry about using a fake name. I used that name on my profile when I was married, but there's no need to lie any more."

"How long have you been divorced?"

"About nine months now. I came out to her a month before the divorce. I think she knew already but she still tried to make it work - even after I told her."

"How long have you known you were gay?"

"I think I knew in some way, shape, or form when I hit puberty and sex entered the brain."

"But you got married any way."

"I come from a *very* Catholic family with loads of brothers and sisters. In our family, when you hit your twenties, you get married and you make babies. Thankfully my wife and I could never conceive. I would have hated explaining this sort of situation to any child of mine."

"I can't imagine what that would be like."

"So Tom's your real name right?"

"It's actually 'Thomas'. 'Tom' is just an alias I use when I meet strangers from the Internet."

"Very funny. I guess I deserve it."

"Don't worry about it, *Andy*."

Andy smiled, opened his water bottle, and drank half of it immediately. "Anyway, sorry for being late. Someone came to my house to buy some furniture I listed online."

"*Another* Internet hookup? I'm impressed."

"Who said anything about this being a hookup? Something tells me you've got something on your mind..."

"I hate to disappoint you, but I really don't. What's on my mind is freedom - I don't have to return to work for another ten weeks."

"To freedom!" Andy raised his bottle and drank the rest, panting as he finished.

"So what kind of sights did you want to see?" Tom asked.

"Well, since moving here I haven't really strayed from the 4-block radius around my house. It's that one across the street and down a few." He pointed to a small modernized ranch-style house with a large covered porch. "With the grocery store nearby I've not had to really leave the area for anything. To be frank, I'd like to see something that reflects the energy of the area- you know, something authentic. Minor aesthetic differences aside, all towns big and small have the same shops and basic attractions. I'd like to see what makes this place different."

"I think I know just the place. I can drive if you'd like."

"I really would. There's nothing like getting a local to show you the real beating heart of an area."

Tom drank what was left of his coffee in one gulp then left a small tip on the table before showing Andy out to his car. As Tom started the engine, a Broken Social Scene record immediately began blaring from the stereo. Tom quickly turned the volume down and Andy's face lit up.

"Oh wow I've not heard this in ages! Is this their first one?"

"Yeah, *Feel Good Lost*. A friend gave it to me a couple years ago for my birthday. He wrote a little note saying that there's nothing better to do on a hot summer afternoon than put this album on, curl up in bed with the windows open, and have a siesta."

"I can imagine," Andy said smiling widely, just like his online profile picture. "So where are we going?"

"Well, it was going to be a surprise - but I'm taking you to my sex dungeon. If you behave, I'll feed you this week."

Andy's eyes widened and he let out a laugh that shook the car. "I had a feeling you were nuts. At least you're funny."

"Oh I'm really glad you said 'funny'. I have a horrible sense of humor and don't really know when and when not to use it. Family gatherings can get a bit awkward."

"Must be nice though to be in touch with your family though."

"Do you talk much to yours?"

"My mom died when I was seventeen and my dad and I haven't talked since I got divorced and told him I was gay."

"That's horrible."

"I expected it really."

"Any siblings?"

"Yeah, but I'm not even sure if my brothers and sisters know about my divorce. Once we all got married, we never really stayed in touch. Everyone has their own lives, their own kids. We only really used to meet up for family gatherings, but when Mom died, Dad kept to himself."

Tom quickly changed the subject. "I've got to ask - why Belton?"

"A few years ago, I was asked to give a speech at a conference at here. As I drove down Main Street trying to find my hotel, I ended up falling in love with the place. It seemed to have the right balance of old-fashioned sensibility and the modern conveniences I'm used to. When the divorce went through late last year, my wife and I decided to continue living at our house until we could sell it. I don't know why, but the day the house sold something compelled me to look online for houses in Belton. I went online and found this house right away at a ridiculously low price. I put an offer in and got the house nine hours after the one in Houston sold. It all felt like fate."

"Or dumb luck."

"Or dumb luck."

"So what do you do for a living?" Tom asked.

"Nothing at the moment, but I used to be a lawyer."

"Oh wow."

"I was a real nasty one too - the Nineties really brought out the worst of me. I turned into this Gordon Gekko-slash-Patrick Bateman prick who'd screw anyone over for a win."

"You said you *used* to be a lawyer - what made you stop?"

"One day I was out for lunch and bumped into someone I knew from a case. Her husband lost his arm from the shoulder down in a factory accident and I defended the factory in a liability case. After digging around, I was able to prove that the accident happened a few minutes beyond this guy's scheduled hours. Because he didn't clock back in on time after his shift, he was there on his own time and the factory only had to pay minimal damages."

"Shit."

"That night, after the ruling, my boss took me out on the town and we drank and snorted anything in front of us. The next day I went out for a sandwich and saw this woman on the street. As we walked past each other, I recognized her straight away and she definitely recognized me. I mean, how could she forget me? Whatever I took the night before was still in my system and it made me feel sickeningly paranoid. When I saw her turn around and walk right up to me, I expected her to stab me in the gut, push me into traffic, or at the very least slap me across the face. Instead she just stood in front of me, looked me in the eyes as I quivered, and said, 'I'll pray for you Mr. Strauss.' I walked straight back to work and quit."

"We're here," Tom said.

Andy was so involved in telling his tale that he paid no attention to the drive nor to his current surroundings. Tom stopped in a small parking lot in what looked like a sparse, anemic park built in the 1960s and untouched since. Everything - gazebos, benches, tables, fenceposts, playground equipment - was made of reinforced concrete and rusting sheet metal. As Andy bewilderedly stepped out of the car, he scanned his surroundings and shook his head.

"*This* is what you wanted to show me?"

"Come this way."

Andy's flip-flops clapped as he followed Tom through a creaking chain-link gate and down a gravel path while tall, wispy grasses tickled his calves and ankles. The path led up to a colossal grassy hill with a striking line of cedar trees behind it; only the sharp tips of the trees' crowns showed. At the apex of the hill, Andy realized they had been walking towards the precipice of a massive dam with cars driving quickly along the top. To their right was a large lake previously obscured by the trees.

"In the Sixties the Army Corps of Engineers dammed up the Lampasas River, creating this huge lake. Usually it's quite picturesque from here, but thanks to a drought the water level is pretty damn low. The shores have dried up quite a bit making the place look a bit otherworldly." Tom pointed across the lake towards a cliff face. "About twenty miles west from here is an Army base called Fort Hood. They built it in the Second World War, and since then the Army's been the main influence on everything that happens here. The nearby towns expanded as the soldiers came making the old landowners very wealthy. You can still see their names on some of the major roads and neighborhoods. In times of relative peace the economy here booms, but when the soldiers are sent off to fight we slide into recession. There's not really much of a native culture to speak of as so many of the residents are so transient. Most of the locals here are still only first- or second-generation military."

"Were your family in the military?"

"On both sides my grandfathers were in the Army but they ended up settling here. My parents stuck around until just a few years ago, but I was born and raised here." A breeze blew Tom's hair onto his face as he looked out on the water.

Andy said, "Usually on the dating site, you come across loads of bland guys with pictures of them half-naked, staring blankly into a camera they're holding up to a mirror. If you're lucky you get to see them totally naked." He laughed heartily at his own joke. "But if you're really lucky you get to meet someone interesting who treats you like a human being instead of just another lay."

"Oh, stop it Mike."

Andy rolled his eyes.

"So what did you do once you quit being a lawyer?"

"I went into charities and fundraising."

Tom furrowed his brow and said, "That seems like a pretty sharp change."

"I wasn't doing it purely out of the goodness of my heart - there's serious money to be made in charity. I worked for an organization that dealt with fraternities and other university societies. As their representative, I was in charge of wining-and-dining prospective donors as well as chasing up alumni and asking for their donations. Basically I would schmooze and guilt people into giving me money."

A fat red squirrel dropped from one of the cedar trees and briefly stared at Tom and Andy before running back up the tree.

"This place really is lovely. In Houston, the nicest landscapes we have are pine forests scattered amongst the swamps. The water in the bay is pretty polluted and the beaches are pretty rank. I have a personal policy where I avoid any beach that has designated showers for washing off tar. Galveston's nice though. At least there you can walk on the beach barefoot."

"That's where my parents live now."

"Oh nice. Why'd they move?"

"I think they just wanted a change. Dad was fed up being fed up at work and Mom was fed up with Dad being fed up. They only have a few more years before they can retire but they practically live as retirees already. They seem much happier there."

"Do you keep in touch?"

"Not as much as I should. In fact my mom's in town today visiting my sister and her kids. They want me to come by but I just wanted some time to myself."

"How's that working out?"

Tom smirked and said, "Quite well actually."

"You really should go see your mother. Trust me, if you're not in touch now you'll regret it later on."

"You're right. I'll see her tomorrow I guess. There's a party at my sister's for her friends and a couple of our cousins. Hey, would you want to come with me tomorrow?"

"What - like a date?"

Oh, what the hell. "Okay, let's call it a date. The thing is, my sister's not so keen on the gay thing. She goes to one of the local evangelical churches and tried pushing me to attend one of those gay-conversion camps. It might be easier for everyone involved if we say we're friends and avoid her lunacy. Would that be alright with you?"

"Fine by me. What time?"

"I could pick you up at two on my way there."

"Sounds great. Gotta ask, do your parents know you're gay?"

"I'm not sure. It's never been brought up in conversation but we don't really talk that often. They've never been introduced to any boyfriends and we never talk about my love life - or lack thereof."

"You know, 'out of sight, out of mind' only works for so long."

"It's worked for us so far."

They walked back to Tom's car and drove back to Andy's house. Tom parked under a large pecan tree in Andy's front yard; the unripe grey-green husks of its fruit hung down in clusters and scantly dotted the manicured lawn. Tom followed Andy up the steps and watched as he bashfully fumbled through his keys, trying several before getting the right one. Inside, dozens of boxes were scattered about and the few skewed pieces of furniture were labeled with orange paper tags marked with numbers. Even though a thin film of unsettled dust seemed to cover every surface and the dark hardwood floors creaked throughout the house, Tom still found Andy's house rather charming. After a brief tour, Tom turned down Andy's offer for a drink and excused himself for the evening. Andy warmly hugged Tom and thanked him at the front door as he left.

Physically and mentally drained, Tom immediately began running a bath when he returned home. He undressed in front of a full-length mirror in his hallway as the tub filled, gratifyingly throwing each wadded piece of work clothing towards the laundry basket in his room. Tom stared at the increasingly foggy mirror with a frown, scrutinizing his nude body exactly as he had done every day for the past few years. Over time, the same light from the same small recessed bulbs formed different shadows over soft new ridges and valleys. The subtle arrival of unfamiliar textures and sparse, anomalous hairs on his trunk never failed to unsettle Tom. He turned sideways, pinching a pale bit of skin above his left hipbone, then sucked in his belly and flexed his biceps, trying his hardest to remember them at their best.

You're going for a run tomorrow.

Tom's shoulders compressed inwards and his knees sharply bent as he slid his large frame into the small tub, allowing the warm water to cocoon over his torso and neck. There were no children to teach, teachers to coddle, or distractions to disregard here - only sweet refuge. Tom felt himself slowly drift into a blissful state of languid detachment. By ten, the bathwater had gone tepid and Tom went straight to bed after drying himself off, falling asleep just as he pulled the covers to his chin.

6

Tom's phone rang at 10:27. He didn't set an alarm but still felt guilty for oversleeping.

"Hi Kate."

"Tom, I slept with him again." Tom sighed loudly. "His parents were still gone so we arranged to meet up. I lied and told my sister I was going out with a few teachers for end-of-year drinks and she agreed to watch the boys. I ended up staying over at his place and when I woke up I felt terrible. We were in his room with his trophies and video games and his dirty laundry, and I realized it looked a bit too much like my own sons' rooms. I told him I had to pick the boys up and left right away."

"Do you think he noticed you were uneasy?"

"Did he hell! He's twenty-one! *Boys* his age don't pick up on things like that. I bet he was still delirious having slept with a former teacher."

"God, if I could sleep with some of my teachers from the past... Mr. McLean from pre-algebra. NO! Mr. Donalds from geography! What a stud..." Tom squirmed and crossed his legs under the blanket as he thought about his former schoolboy crushes.

"Sorry to lay this on you. I just needed to talk to someone. I'm going to take a shower and head over to my sister's. Are you coming to the graduation ceremony tonight?"

"I've got a family thing at Sam's. I'd invite you but I don't want anyone getting hurt."

41

"Understood. Sam still a bitch?"

"She's getting better. Honestly, I think the divorce was the best thing to happen to her since Shelley was born. I've not been the brunt of any judgmental rants in a while now."

"That's good."

"I met up with that guy yesterday."

"*Tell me everything.*"

"Well, there's really not much to tell. We met up for a quick coffee, I took him to the park at the dam, and then I dropped him off at his house."

"That's it? Was he ugly or something?"

"No, not at all. He's kinda cute actually. He's a bit older than me, wavy brown hair, about five-ten -"

"How much older?"

"Dunno, I'd guess about ten years or so."

"Does it bother you?"

"I don't think so. I haven't really thought about it much, but I figure I either have a connection with someone or I don't. Age is incidental."

"So when are you seeing him again?"

"What makes you so sure know I will?"

"Call it a woman's intuition."

"I'm taking him to my sister's this afternoon."

"What?! I didn't think you moved that fast!"

"He's the one who talked me into even going to Sam's in the first place. Plus, my mom's up from Galveston."

"Oh wow, so you're going to introduce him to your mom too?"

"Just as a friend. I don't want to start a riot."

"I bet that makes him feel real special. Anyway, I really need to get moving. Have fun today. Oh - and let me know when you two set a date for your nuptials. I'll see if I can arrange a bachelorette party for you."

"You can always get your young stud to strip for me."

"Bye Tom."

Despite being ferociously hungry, Tom forced himself to go out for a run before the heat would be unbearable. Tom's lungs and sinuses ached and burned as he ran past dozens of lawns being mown by men in baseball caps and sunglasses, groups of children yelling and throwing footballs in the street, and several pairs of religious proselytizers sweating as they swarmed through the neighborhood, desperately trying to catch people at home. Despite the abundance of stimuli, Tom's mind was blank aside from a heightened physical self-awareness of the endorphins coursing through his body and a calm, intangible harmony with his surroundings. His normal anxieties of work, family, love, money, and the unexpected only briefly surfaced in his mind as rough, sketchy abstracts that vanished as quickly as they appeared.

Tom walked straight to his kitchen after his short run and quaffed the remaining half-carton of orange juice from the fridge. Tom's sweat-drenched sports top clung to his chest and turned cold as he stood in front of the open refrigerator door. He again stripped off his clothes in front of the hallway mirror and his eyes were immediately drawn to an old scar on his left arm that had turned bright red after the run. After showering, Tom prepared a large bowl of muesli and Greek yogurt with a drizzle of honey then sat down at the dining table with a Don DeLillo novel he received from Jeremy months ago as a birthday present. Tom had been saving the book for his vacation and imagined himself reading it while sunbathing on a beach somewhere.

There's still time.

Just after one o'clock, Tom set the book down and left to pick up Andy. As he neared the house, Tom saw Andy outside wearing a sleeveless shirt and basketball shorts as he loaded a low bookshelf into a woman's minivan. She backed out of the driveway after handing Andy a check and continued scowling as she drove past Tom. The back of her van was absolutely covered in religious and right-wing political bumper stickers.

"Sorry I'm early. She seemed *interesting*."

Andy rolled his eyes. "Yeah, well, when I said I needed to hurry up for a date, she asked what my date was like and wasn't too thrilled to find out it was a man. She didn't say a word to me after that. ... Do we need to go straight away?"

"There's no rush, honest. I do need to pick up some ice on the way."

"Right, I'll be ready in two minutes."

"I'll wait out here."

As Andy jogged inside through the double garage door, Tom walked into the shade of the pecan tree and a cool gust of wind blew down the open neck of his shirt. Tom knew these breezes would only last a couple more weeks before the relentless heat would take over until September. He worked his fingertips into the grooves of the rough, scaly bark and traced their furrows before pulling his hand away and digging specks of blue-black dirt from his fingernails.

Tom's sister Sam lived in Morgan's Point Resort, a small town on the shore of Belton Lake. Six miles outside the city limits, Tom pulled off the main farm-to-market road into the unpaved parking lot of a tiny convenience store. The tattered shop had been in business for as long as Tom could remember. Many of the decayed whitewashed wood panels moved with the wind, pulling away and towards the wall like slits on a fish's gill. Sets of long-dead Christmas lights dangled from the corners of the building to adjacent lampposts. Two disused gas pumps with folding numerical displays baked and rusted underneath a sign that read 'BAIT' in bright red letters. Tom and Andy entered the shop, no bigger than Tom's living room, and the walls shook as the door slammed behind them. Their faces contorted as they were hit with a concentrated wall of smells of festering fish, coffee, cleaning solution, and freshly popped popcorn. Tom brought the kids' favorite sweets and two large bags of ice to the counter where a teenage boy tapped away on his laptop.

"You fellas need anything else?" the boy asked.

Andy said, "Yeah - I'd like an order of bait worms please."

Tom stared at Andy bewilderedly.

"Small or large, sir?"

"Just a small one thanks."

The boy disappeared under the counter and returned seconds later with a small styrofoam tub.

That's the same tub my local BBQ joint uses for their sauce.

"That's $10.83 please."

"Do you take card?"

The boy looked puzzled and stared at Andy with an annoyed look of disbelief. "Of course we take card - this IS America!"

The men took their items and left the store. They both flinched as the door shut noisily behind them.

"Andy, why the hell did you buy those worms?"

"We were in a bait shop and I've never bought bait before. I figured I might as well."

"What were you planning on doing with them?"

"No idea really. Maybe I'll go fishing. Never done that before either."

Tom briefly recalled cold, early morning fishing trips with his father and Sam. About twice a year they drove to a collapsed bridge on the Lampasas River with sandwiches and sports drinks. Tom never caught anything big enough to keep. "I just ask that when we get to Sam's house you leave the worms outside of my car in the shade. I don't want them stinking up my car."

"Do they really stink?" Andy's eyebrows raised in astonishment as he lifted the lid of the tub to see a compressed, writing mass of sludge. He brought the tub to his nose and gagged, nearly spilling the container as Tom drove back onto the main road.

"Is that red stuff in the tub blood?!"

"I always assumed it was."

"Oh God, that's disgusting!" Andy laughed heartily, his chest shuddering with each uninhibited giggle. Tom couldn't help but laugh along as he glanced over at the overgrown kid sitting next to him with worms in one hand and candy in the other.

Tom turned off down a hilly, wooded road marked with a sign that read '*The U.S. Army Corps of Engineers, Fort Worth District welcomes you to Belton Lake*'. Several cars were parked outside Sam's house and white balloons were tied to her large bricked mailbox. Sam met her fiancé while she was still married to her first husband, and while nobody knew for sure, there were rumors of infidelity on her part. Weeks after her divorce, Sam moved in to her fiancée's house with the kids. The children were thrilled when they heard they'd be moving in with Tom but were crushed when they learned it was the wrong one.

Inside the house were some of Sam's friends from high school that stayed local. As adults they treated Tom well but when they were all younger, Sam's friends tormented Tom at any given opportunity. Their favorite prank was to lock him in the tool shed and call him 'sissy' and 'faggot' until he cried - the usual little brother upbringing. Tom assumed that by now everyone knew he was gay and now that he arrived with another man, he assumed that they assumed Andy was his boyfriend.

Tom and Andy entered the house without knocking and went straight to the kitchen. Tom's mother Anne stood by the fridge with a glass of iced tea.

"Hi Mom!"

"Come here and give me a hug! Your father has a golf tournament this weekend so I thought I might as well come up to see everyone. Who's this?"

Andy held his hand out to Tom's mother. "I'm Andy. Nice to meet you."

She raised an eyebrow and grinned. "Hello Andy, I'm Anne. It's nice to meet you too. Tom's never mentioned you before."

Tom spoke up. "Andy's a friend of mine who's just moved to the area from Houston."

"How did you two meet?"

Andy quickly said, "I've been selling some furniture I don't need and Tom bought a bookshelf from me."

"Tom, honey, don't you have enough books and bookshelves? I mean, I'm happy you're not hooked on drugs or dressing up for the Renaissance Faire, but you can't spend your whole life in books. You should get out there and meet some people. Live your life, baby."

"Tom's been kind enough to show me around the area. I still don't have my bearings yet but he's already shown me the lakes. I really love the place."

"The lakes are lovely, especially when the water level's higher. So what moved you up here from Houston? Do you have family here?" Tom felt himself lightly perspire.

"No family. Actually, I've recently divorced and moved up here to start fresh."

"I totally understand - we moved to Galveston for a fresh start. Tom's father Jim nearly worked himself crazy at the hospital in Temple. Jim's a sensitive soul and just couldn't switch off his brain between work and home so we decided it would be best to transfer to a less stressful position. Thankfully there was an opening in Galveston and he took it."

"My wife and I used to regularly visit Galveston. Four years back when Hurricane Ike hit, we were stranded there a few days due to the flooding."

"That was really scary for Jim and me. We're used to

47

tornadoes and really bad thunderstorms but there's something terrifying about the slow approach of a hurricane."

Sam walked into the kitchen holding a plastic sandcastle bucket with one of the turrets cracked off. "When I invited you I didn't think you'd actually show up. Still it's good to see you. Who's this?"

Anne moved in between Sam and Andy. "This is Andy, Tom's friend. He's just moved here from Houston."

Sam shook Andy's hand. "You've never mentioned him before, Tom."

Andy said, "I've actually just moved up this last week."

"Well at least Tom's made a new friend. I've not met any of his friends since that Kate woman from work. There was something I really didn't like about her." *Maybe it was that she was a woman and I wasn't dating her?* "Do you still work with her?"

Tom said, "Yeah but we've all just split up for the summer break until August."

"Oh yeah I forgot you're off work for so long? Any plans?"

"Nothing yet. I was thinking about showing up to the airport with a packed suitcase and going somewhere to escape the heat."

"Well that's stupid," Sam said throwing her arms in the air. "You should organize something like that. I'll give you some brochures of places Tom and I were looking at."

"I think it sounds like good fun," Anne said. "No offense honey, but it doesn't sound like something you'd do."

"I know. It was an idea I had a few months ago but I've not really done much about it."

"Sounds like the act itself would be all that's required. There's nothing stopping you. Do you have enough money saved up?"

"I've got enough set aside." Tom's simple, single life let him save up quite a bit of money even after paying off his student loans.

"Well I say go for it."

Tom's niece Shelley saw him through the sliding glass door and screamed "UNCLE TOM'S HERE!" as she ran towards the house. Her shriek seemed to get louder each time Tom visited.

"UNCLE TOM! UNCLE TOM! I MISSED YOU!"

Tom glanced over at Andy as he laughed at Shelley's unwitting reference. Anne started to giggle too and in seconds the pair of them were red in the face.

"I have something for you, Shelley."

"Candy! Candy!"

Tom handed her a small box of lemon drops. Her face puckered and smiled as she placed one of the sweets on her tongue. The little girl touched her lips twice and Tom bent down to kiss her. She giggled and ran into a back bedroom.

"Tom, I told you to stop bringing them sweets all the time," Sam said.

"Yeah but look how happy she is. More importantly, listen... No screaming."

"UNCLE TOM! UNCLE TOM!" Brandon came running down the hallway with a lemon drop in his mouth. Anne and Andy creased with laughter.

"Now Brandon, you shouldn't run with candy in your mouth. You could choke on it. You don't want to hurt yourself, do you?"

Brandon shook his head and held his arms out for a hug. As Tom leaned in he whispered a soft "shhh" in the boy's ear and handed him a small bag of gummy bears. The plastic wrapper loudly crinkled as Brandon tried to slyly slide the candy in his pocket. The adults pretended not to notice.

"Who are you?" Brandon asked.

"I'm Andy. I'm a friend of Uncle Tom's." Andy gently bit his lower lip to keep from laughing.

"You're a lot shorter than Uncle Tom."

"Lots of people are. He's a pretty tall guy."

"Yeah he is. Sometimes when we're playing he turns into a big, scary monster that picks me up and tries to hold me up to the lights to melt me. Then he tries to eat my belly and it tickles. I always beat him though. I shoot him with my laser guns and he falls down and shakes."

"He sounds like a pretty weak monster."

Brandon scratched his head. "No, he's really strong. I'm just smarter than him. You gotta use your brains to beat the big guys."

"Or your laser guns."

"Or my laser guns." Brandon smiled and pulled imaginary guns from holsters on his sides. He fired several loud, sizzling rounds into the air that fried the ceiling fan and drywall above. His candy fell out of his
pocket to the ground and Brandon holstered his weapons to pick up the sweet, precious bounty. With the spoils of war secured, he ran out of the room to play outside.

"Bye Uncle Tom! Bye Uncle Andy!"

Tom looked at Andy with slight horror as Sam and Anne laughed. They all watched through the window as Brandon shot the other Tom dead with his laser guns.

After Sam took everyone outside to meet the rest of the guests, the Toms walked away to a quiet corner of the backyard and talked about Sam's obsessive wedding organization while Andy sampled the buffet with Anne.

"I've been out of the Army for 4 years now and feel like I'm living with my old drill sergeant!"

"Hush! If she hears us she'll make us clean the back patio with our toothbrushes!"

Sam shot them a glance that instantly shut them up.

"Seriously though, no matter what Sam says, your 'Plus One' is for whoever you want to bring. She'll bitch and moan about condoning homosexuality in a church but she forgets that this is my wedding too. Hell, it's my first wedding so I damn well have a say in what happens."

"Thanks Tom. It means a lot to me."

"So are you seeing this Andy guy?"

"Sort of. I don't know. I only really met him yesterday afternoon. Technically, this is our first date."

"And it took you so long to introduce him to the family?"

"Please don't start. Andy's a really nice guy but I barely know him. He's starting his life from scratch and has only recently came out of the closet. In fact, please don't tell Sam or Mom that he's gay. I don't want them jumping to any conclusions. Still, Andy's good company and I really get along with him. I'm not really used to having gay male friends that I *don't* sleep with... Sorry you probably don't really want to hear about that."

"No, no it's cool. It's pointless to avoid talking about stuff between friends just because I'm straight and you're gay - even if it is about sex. We're both guys talking about the exact same thing."

"Too true. Everyone's okay with talking about murder and child abuse in the news or watching gory violence and rape in films, but mention gay sex and *you're* the pervert. Makes you worry about a culture with standards like that."

"Anyway, the wedding is only two weeks away. If you're still seeing Andy, please bring him. Everyone seems to like the guy."

They looked over at Andy chatting with Sam and one of her neighbors. All three of them laughed as Andy wildly gesticulated towards the fence and the roof in the middle of a story. Shelley ran up to them and loudly joined in the laughter, oblivious to the situation.

The long-drawn-out summer sunset began as Tom and Andy stood at Sam's front door carrying bags and plastic containers grotesquely full of food. Judging by the amount, Tom guessed that they could eat nothing but what they carried for the next three days and still have leftovers. *Such are families*, Tom thought.

"Sam, Anne - it was really lovely to meet you both." Andy kissed the women on their cheeks and waved as he walked to the car.

Sam waited for the passenger door to close before saying, "It's nice that you have actual people friends now."

"Thanks Sam. I'll let him know that you consider him an actual person. I'm sure it will make his day."

Anne put her hand on Tom's shoulder. "Tom honey, please come down to Galveston and visit your father and me some time soon. With all the tropical flowers blooming this time of the year, it's easy to forget you're in Texas."

"I'll see what I can do." He hugged her and kissed her on the cheek.

"It really is good to see you," Sam said. "You seem a lot less gloomy."

"I'll take that as a compliment."

"Sorry. You know what I mean. Take care little brother."

"You too Sam. Give my best to Tom." They hugged and Tom walked to the car. For Tom, leaving a family gathering without feeling enervated was a new concept. As he walked to the car he noticed Andy had been watching from the passenger seat. As if a compulsory act, Tom drooped his head and tried to look battered and fatigued.

"Sorry about that. I know how tiring my family can be."

"Are you kidding? I think they're great - and what brilliant kids! I wish my family was as personal."

"I guess it's a bit different now. Sam's getting married soon and Mom's getting excited. She hated Sam's first husband and warned her not to get married just because she was pregnant. There's always been a quiet I-told-you-so in the air but they're a lot better these days."

"Thanks for taking me today."

"No, seriously, thank you for coming. With you there I think they finally believe I'm human!"

Tom's compact sedan groaned as it slowly crawled up and over the hills leaving the lakeside. Tom and Andy rolled the windows down and let the car and their ears fill with the rushing evening wind.

Across town at the convention center, Susan Ortega stood at the side of a carpeted stage as her name was called over the booming applause of nearly two thousand people and the drone of 'Pomp and Circumstance'. Susan's blue gown flowed as she walked to the end of the stage where the principal stood next to a large pile of blank mock diplomas. She strolled up to the principal, shook his hand with the right, and took the mock diploma with the left. To Susan, the simulated display felt like a strange entrance ritual for a club she had no interest in joining. The rest of the ceremony consisted of several Christian prayers and live video feeds from soldiers in Iraq and Afghanistan with a few speeches in between. Predictably, a sea of glossy blue hats were thrown in the air at the end of the convocation but Susan held on to hers. She knew exactly how much the hat cost and didn't dream of losing it. The crowd dispersed and Susan earnestly looked out to the stands to spot her father and brother sitting in a row above an exit sign.

"Hi Daddy! Hi Robby!"

"I'm so proud of you Susan!"

"I'm proud Susan!" Roberto shouted.

Susan smiled didn't see what all the fuss was about. For her, completing school was something that had to be done without questioning.

"Thanks Dad. Are you ready to go?"

"Don't you want to stay around with your friends?"

"Not really. They're all headed off to get wasted. I just want to get home and have something to eat."

"How about I take you out somewhere nice tonight?"

Susan knew how limited their savings were. "All the restaurants will be booked up already. Plus I'm pretty tired. Could we just get a pizza and rent a DVD tonight?"

When her mother died last year, Susan watched firsthand as her father slipped into an emotional paralysis and started drinking heavily. Susan knew how much her mother meant to José and never outwardly criticized his drinking nor his indefinite leave from work. The family was given a large sum of money from Sharon's life insurance policy but most of it went to the debt they had accrued over the years. The amount left was more than enough to cover living expenses for a couple years but José never showed any signs that he'd return to work. To save money, they moved out of their large family house near the hospital to a cheaper apartment building nearer to Roberto's preschool across town. Susan was able to obtain a minor's hardship driving license and managed most of the usual shopping errands.

"Susie - did you hear how loud everyone cheered when your name was called?"

The time between walking up to the stage to the moment Susan saw the tassels of graduation caps spinning in the air was a blur.

"Yeah it was crazy, wasn't it. Did you see Mr. Woodbine anywhere?"

"Sorry sweetie - I wasn't really looking."

The Ortega family spent a normal night together sat around the television. After eating, Roberto and José laid across the sofa asleep as *E.T.* played on their big-screen television, its display covering nearly half the wall on which it hung. The large pieces of furniture and appliances from their house further crowded the already claustrophobic apartment. Susan felt Roberto lightly snore as she let him doze for a few minutes with his head rested on her lap before she carried him to bed. As she collected the paper plates from the coffee table and switched off the television, Susan looked back at her sleeping father with a sympathy that had calloused over time. After Susan quietly tidied the room, she turned off the lights and walked to her room, looking out her window at the parking lot for Mr. Woodbine's car, but it wasn't there. She changed into her pajamas, climbed into bed, and fell asleep easily as she always did. Minutes later, she began to dream.

Susan stands alone on the convention center stage wearing her graduation cap and gown, gazing out towards the audience. Glaring back is a horde of thousands, maybe millions of madly flashing cameras. The blinding wall of light burns Susan's eyes and she quickly turns away covering her face. Facing the other way, she wipes her eyes and dazedly looks up to see her shadow stretched to fit the massive satin-draped backdrop. Susan stays still, watching her shadow twitch and convulse to the unceasing glimmer of the infinite bulbs. The flashes suddenly stop and the alien sound of silence seems to fill the cavernous room - but the silhouette remains, still shuddering. Susan raises and lowers her arms to try to make the hulking shadow react but it stays stationary. Curious and slightly afraid, she walks up to the drapes and reaches out to the figure with her right hand - which feels cold and wet to the touch - and a wave of anger and sadness overtakes Susan. She punches the curtains and screams at the silhouette with all her might, but no sound comes out of her mouth. The shadow stays perfectly motionless. Susan closes her eyes and turns around to face the audience. As she opens her eyes, all that remains is a white coffin on a stand surrounded by yellow roses in the middle of the auditorium.

Susan woke with her hands held up to her stinging eyes and quickly realized she had been crying in her sleep. Thinking of the long Sunday ahead of her, she flipped her damp pillow over and laid staring at the ceiling praying for slumber.

8

They stood outside Andy's house just as darkness fell.

"Tom, would you like to come in for a drink?"

Tom said, "Well I -"

"Oh come on. You look like you could use one."

Don't be such a bore. "Oh alright." Just saying this aloud made Tom feel loose in the knees.

"Great! Just bear with me for a couple moments, OK?"

Andy used the screen of his phone as a flashlight as he fumbled through his keys in the dark. After removing his shoes at the door, he jogged past Tom towards one of the back bedrooms with a wide-eyed, boyish energy. Tom walked to the kitchen and chuckled as he listened to Andy noisily rummage through boxes. yAndy returned holding a dusty black champagne bottle and two crystal flutes.

"I was going to wait for my fifteenth wedding anniversary with my wife but I really can't think of a better time than now to drink it."

"This is too much Andy, really."

"Nonsense. I've waited far too long for this." Andy picked up the bottle. "It took me a month after coming out to convince my wife that I couldn't go back to living a lie." He peeled off the black foil covering the cork. "It took me another nine months to settle all the legal aspects of the divorce and sell the house." He unravelled and removed the cork's wire cage. "And it took me a week to mentally adjust to this new place before I actually ventured out - and that's thanks to you." He pointed the bottle towards the living room. "But most of all, it took me forty-five years to be able to stand up and live my own life."

The cork shot across the open plan kitchen/dining room with a bang and bounced off the ceiling before landing behind some boxes marked 'SHEETS'. Andy smiled more intensely and sincerely than Tom had yet seen.

Andy poured the champagne and shouted, "To freedom!" while raising his glass.

Tom, stunned, picked up his glass and repeated, "To freedom!"

After clinking glasses, Andy swished the champagne in his mouth and his smile quickly faded. "You know, I mentally built this moment up so much and hoped this champagne would taste orgasmic. Instead it just tastes like decent champagne. I'm a little disappointed."

"I think you must have a dirty glass because mine is definitely orgasmic."

Andy smirked and said, "I think it's just because somewhere deep down I hoped that everything would look different, and that I'd start feeling like a different person with a different lease on life."

"And how do you feel?"

Andy scratched the top of his head and said, "I feel like something in me has changed a tiny bit, but the world around me still looks and feels the same. And I can't tell if that little bit that's changed has done so because I've moved *here* or because I've left *there* - or even just because I've willed it."

"Can I give you a little advice?"

"Please!"

"With all this change happening around you, don't expect to fully understand everything right away. Hindsight will make things clearer over time."

"That doesn't help much."

"Of course it doesn't, not now at least. You have to give this time."

"Thanks I guess."

Andy walked to the living room and placed a record on his turntable. At the first drum strike of 'Running Up That Hill', Tom began to laugh.

"What's so funny? I thought you liked Kate Bush."

"Oh I do," Tom said wincing. "It's just that this album has a weird significance for me."

"I can see you squirming - this will be good! Hold that thought!" Andy ran to the kitchen for the champagne and his glass then threw himself down at the sofa. "Mr. Woodbine, spill your guts!"

Tom walked to the living room stepping in time with the song. "Okay. When I was twenty, just a few weeks after I came out, I went to this incredible record store in Austin called Waterloo Records and this song came on the store's sound system. I had never heard any Kate Bush stuff before and was immediately hooked. The music got my toe tapping right away and then her incredible voice came in. I had no idea what or who she was singing about, but I knew I had to have the record. The cashier didn't know the record so he called his manager over. Now, at that age, I'd never knowingly been checked out by a guy - but I knew right away that the way the manager looked at me could only mean one thing."

"What was he like?"

"He was only a few years older than me, but he had this weird, 1960s Austin hippie vibe about him. His whole look was deliberately scraggly and unprocessed. He walked me over to the Kate Bush records and showed me the *Hounds of Love* album. I remember seeing the cover and thinking that Kate looked a lot like my mother in the Eighties. Anyway, this guy told me all about her other albums and some of the background information about this one, but by then I wasn't even listening. I just grabbed the records and followed him back over to the cash register. As he gave me the change, he handed me his number and invited me out that night. The club we went to was really cheesy, but everyone there knew it was and put on no pretenses about the place. After a few drinks, he started complaining about the music and we went back to his place - which was surreal. There was just enough room for his bed, a sofa, a table, and his records - nothing else. We opened some beers and he rifled through his insanely big record collection for this one. We fooled around on his sofa a bit and then we really got into it once the drums really kicked in. He didn't know - or at least I think he didn't know - but I lost my virginity to him. I look back on the whole thing with unease and a bit of regret because we weren't protected. He didn't once mention it and I was just too naïve and caught up in the moment to even think about it. I was lucky that nothing came of it."

"So you lost your virginity to Kate Bush howling about clouds?"

"The best part was when he stopped groping me just as side A finished, then leapt from the sofa and ran to flip the record. The rest of the album is really strange and broody and set a weird mood."

"I bet. Here's a fun question: have you ever slept with a woman?"

"Almost. I dated a couple girls in high school and college, but I broke up with them when sex became unavoidable. I just couldn't go through with it." Tom glanced over and watched Andy as he reached and placed his glass on the coffee table next to a bound notebook. Tom peered through a small opening in between the buttons on Andy's shirt to his solar plexus. A small trail of dark brown hair tracked from his chest down to his stomach.

In a perfectly affected English accent Andy asked, "Would you like some more champagne, sir?"

payment sense.

0845 434 6001

payment sense.

0845 434 6001

STEM

WC1B 2LF

Thank You

M:5203345095190939

TID:16799199   5975

HANDSET:1

MASTERCARD

AID: A0000000041010

MasterCard

5187 9104 3430 4654

EXP 04/21

PAN SEQ NO:33

STT 02/17

ICC009 tCK SPBD

SALE

AMOUNT

TOTAL   £142.32

PIN VERIFIED

02/10/18 21:36

AUTH CODE:F18135

TXN 0835

MERCHANT COPY

PLEASE RETAIN RECEIPT

Tom replied in kind. "Pour dear boy, pour!"

As they quickly finished the bottle of champagne, Andy described the lies he told his wife about non-existing work appointments to meet up with men in the evenings. For the last couple years of their marriage, he and his wife hardly spent any time together.

"Do you think she had any affairs?"

"I don't know, but a big part of me hopes so. If anything it's the thought of her being unhappy that bothers me the most."

"Has she met anyone since the divorce?"

"No clue - we haven't kept in touch. ... What do you say to another bottle of wine?"

"Oh, go on then."

As Andy skipped to the kitchen, Tom said, "Just to be clear Andy - I'm not sleeping with you."

Andy stopped mid-step and turned to Tom with a hurt look. "What makes you think I want to sleep with you?"

"Sorry, that was supposed to be a joke. I didn't mean anything by it."

"Well thank god for that! Let's get hammered!"

Tom frowned and glared at Andy as he skipped back into the living room carrying a bottle of sauvignon blanc.

"Look," Andy said, putting his hand on Tom's knee. "I didn't invite you in to have sex with you. Yes, I think you're an attractive guy, but you've been nothing but kind and considerate to me from the start and I don't want to fuck that up."

"Thanks Andy." Tom put his hand on Andy's. "That means a lot to me. If you'll excuse me..."

On his walk back from the bathroom, Tom noticed his joints had become looser from the wine and he felt a sway in his step.

"Hey Andy, that champagne has gone straight to my head and I really don't think I should drive. Do you mind if I sleep on your sofa tonight?"

"No problem. I've got some extra blankets and pillows around here somewhere, though you may need to help me find them."

After searching through a few of the boxes, Tom found one that was full of outdoor winter clothes. "Hey Andy, do you ski?"

"The wife and I used to go to Colorado every winter. I really enjoyed it, but looking back I think I preferred ogling men in the jacuzzis at the lodge. With the amount of steam that comes off an outdoor hot tub in a Colorado winter, even the most unremarkable guy on the planet can look like a god as he enters and leaves the water."

Tom visualized sitting in a jacuzzi in the Rockies and watching Andy emerge from the water without clothes. Tom smiled as he realized his daydream reminded him of a slow-motion scene from a tacky music video.

With pillows in his arms, Andy exuberantly turned to Tom and bumped into him, knocking Tom over onto the sofa. Andy tried to catch him but he too was unsteady after the champagne. He landed on top of Tom and his right elbow jabbed into Tom's left thigh.

"JESUS!"

"Oh shit - I'm so sorry! Are you alright?"

"I'm fine, I'm fine... Ow. This is really going to hurt tomorrow. Thank God for wine!"

Andy's face was still wrought with concern. He started backing away from Tom to the other side of the sofa, but just before Andy could sit down, Tom grabbed his right hand. Still in a slump in the corner by the armrest, Tom slowly but decidedly pulled Andy towards him. Andy carefully took Tom's lead, allowing himself to be drawn in. Tom slid back to lay across the sofa and felt his heart pump harder and faster as the skin of their legs touched. Their eyes met and slowly shut as their lips briefly touched. Tom couldn't remember the last time he had been kissed with such consideration. As Tom opened his eyes, he saw Andy laying next to him, smiling widely with his eyes still closed.

"You're something else, Tom. You know, I really didn't intend for this to happen." Andy opened his eyes and flicked his hair away from his face while Tom looked at him with a wary smirk. "I really didn't! But now that it has, I can't pretend I'm not pleased. It is a bit odd to meet a guy online that doesn't immediately try to have sex within minutes of meeting. Plus, I've never met another guy's family before!"

"Oh God - I knew this was coming."

"I kissed your sister *and* your mother before I even kissed you! That's got to be a - "

Tom quickly shut Andy up with a kiss. Tom felt Andy's facial muscles shift into a smile as he ran his hand through Andy's wild hair.

Sunday, May 27

Andy and Tom laid together on the sofa in the early morning hours
and chatted about the graduation ceremony Tom missed that day.

"You sure it's okay that you didn't show up?"

"Yeah, I never go. I try to keep my lives at work and home as separate as possible. Plus I had a family function to attend."

"Yeah but what about your students? Didn't some of them graduate from your class?"

Tom shrugged and said, "They'll all be so worked up by the moment itself that they wouldn't know or care if I showed up."

Andy yawned loudly enough for it to echo down the hallway leading to the front door. The sound surprised them both. Andy stroked Tom's forehead and said, "I'd like to stay up and keep talking but I'm beyond exhausted."

"I'm pretty tired myself."

"You know, you don't have to sleep on the sofa. It's not very comfy."

Tom raised an eyebrow. "What are you trying to say, Mr... Actually, what is your last name?"

"Strauss."

"Are you sure? It's not another fake name is it?"

"Ha-fucking-ha. I'm Andrew Peter Strauss, I was born in Houston on the eighth of June, 1967 -"

"Your birthday's coming up soon!"

"- I wear a size 9 shoe, and my blood type is AB negative. Anything else you want to know?"

"Turn-offs?"

"Piercings, tattoos, really effeminate guys, *man-scaping*... But most of all, smart-asses. Anything else?"

"That's it for now, thanks. So, Mr. Strauss, what were you trying to say about me not having to sleep on the sofa?"

"Well I was trying to say that you're more than welcome to sleep in my bed."

"It's very kind of you to offer your bed, but where will you sleep?"

Andy sat up and rolled his eyes. "You know what I'm trying to say. And look - it's not as if I'm asking you to have sex with me."

"But you are asking me to sleep with you?"

Andy lurched across the sofa at Tom and tickled his sides. In agony, Tom screamed, "Okay! Okay! Enough! ... Can we just go to bed? I'm too tired for any more messing around."

In the bedroom, Andy took off his wristwatch and placed it next to a small leather notebook and gold pen on the bedside table. Tom watched intently as Andy unbuttoned his shirt, gazing at the thick brown hair on his chest that tapered down to a thin trail along his stomach. Tom mentally imagined the sound and feel it would make when twisted between his fingers. Tom instinctively undressed as he watched, mindlessly dropping his clothes to the floor. Still mesmerized, Tom began removing his briefs just as Andy entered the bed still wearing his. The elastic waistband loudly snapped on Tom's skin as he quickly pulled them back on.

"Don't worry - I didn't see anything," Andy said, pulling the sheets up to his chest.

"Sorry, it's just habit."

"It's habit for you to take all your clothes off in front of other men?"

"When I'm getting in bed with one that's already half-naked, yeah."

"Fair enough."

Tom slid under the sheets a few inches away from Andy. They both stayed motionlessly apart for a few moments until Tom turned on his side and shuffled his body back into Andy's to be spooned. Tom felt Andy's body slowly go limp muscle by muscle as he drifted off to sleep. He held on to Andy's right arm, lightly stroking the tiny hairs lining the inside of his elbow, and joined Andy in slumber moments later, dreaming of a barbecue at his sister's house.

Tom is sitting outside with his mother and father and they watch as a dark wall of rain moves toward them from the lake. They run inside where Sam and her kids are sitting around the television. Tom tries to recognize the program but all he hears is the sound of a soprano's aria being slowly drowned out by novelty klaxon buzzers. Sam and Anne start arguing about something from across the room. Their arguing quickly turns into shouting and as they get louder, the rain outside intensifies. The wind seems to be moving nearly horizontally, fiercely blowing leaves and litter against the window. The women launch into a fist fight and Tom's skin begins to burn and tingle. Everyone gasps as Sam strikes Anne in the face and sends her to the floor. Then, with a deafening roar, the house quakes as the roof of the house is savagely ripped apart by a tornado.

Tom's eyes opened widely as he mentally scrambled to find his bearings in this strange new place. Andy's arm was still draped over his chest and Tom realized he must have only been asleep a few minutes. He gently kissed Andy's arm and slid back into a deep, pleasantly dreamless sleep.

9

Andy awoke with a trembling stretch that shook the bed. He looked over just as Tom's face crumpled in a yawn.

"Now there's a good look for you."

It took a couple of seconds for Tom to regain his ability to speak. "Leave me alone you bully."

"No really - the scrunched-up face, the mad hair, the light spittle on the side of your mouth..."

Tom wiped his mouth with his hand and smeared it on Andy's face before grabbing the back of Andy's head and pulling him in for a kiss.

"And to top it off - morning breath!" Andy howled.

Tom glowered and tried to push Andy away, but Andy grabbed Tom's arm and jumped on top of him. They playfully wrestled on the bed and would have fallen off if the blanket hadn't been tangled between Tom's legs. Andy laughed and grabbed Tom by the shoulders, pulling him back to the middle of the bed. As he pinned Tom down on his back, widely grinning in triumph, Tom sheepishly looked down his chest and nodded to suggest Andy should look as well.

"Now *there's* a good look for you, Andy!"

To his horror, Andy looked down and saw he was fully aroused, pulling the elastic band of his briefs slightly away from his waist. Tom bellowed with laughter as Andy flailed to pull the blanket over his face, hiding in humiliation.

"It's alright, Andy. Honestly, don't worry about it. ... Can I tell you something?"

Andy's eyes peered over the blanket. "Yeah."

"I honestly can't remember the last time I've slept with a man."

"But we -"

"No, I know we didn't have sex. I meant that I can't remember actually spending the night with someone then waking up next to him in the morning."

"Oh right."

"And I've definitely never spent the night with a man without having sex."

"Me neither." Andy gently ran his hand along Tom's left arm until reaching a large scar. "What's that from?"

"I was in a car accident back in high school. I was with my friends Jake and Craig on our way to a tennis tournament and we veered off the road just a couple miles away from the sports center. I can't even remember what it was that caused us to swerve, but the car skid down the embankment and started to roll when Craig tried to correct the steering. I was in the backseat and only got this cut and a nasty concussion, but Jake wasn't wearing his seat belt and died almost instantly."

"Jesus!"

"It's really weird, but when I try to think about what happened that day, I feel like my memory keeps changing as time goes by. I don't know why, but I distinctly remember Jake looking back at me after the crash and asking, 'Tom - you okay bro?' I don't remember any of the important details of the crash like what the car looked like before or after the crash, or what the trip in the ambulance was like, or even who came to see me in the hospital, but I distinctly remember Jake turning around in his seat, wearing his white cap and goofy sunglasses, and looking me over to see if I was alright. It was probably the concussion, but even now, just telling you about this memory years later, it feels more real than anything else that happened that day."

After showering, Andy entered the room with a large white towel wrapped around his waist. His skin was slightly pink from the heat of the shower and his hair was still damp, falling onto his forehead and eyebrows.

"I don't want to rush you but I've got someone coming over in about an hour to buy a chair from me. If you hop in the shower, I'll make us some breakfast and we can eat before they get here."

Andy walked over to his dresser and motionlessly stood facing Tom as if to suggest he wasn't going to undress until Tom left the room. As he walked to the bathroom, Tom looked back to the bedroom over his shoulder and saw Andy from behind as he pulled his black briefs up into position.

Tom showered quickly and dried himself off in the bathroom. As he walked back to the bedroom, he heard Andy's loud voice from the kitchen. "I've left you a fresh pair of underwear on the bed. They should fit. Feel free to wear anything from the wardrobe too."

As Tom slipped into a white T-shirt from the wardrobe and buttoned his seersucker shorts, he saw that the leather notebook on Andy's nightstand was laying open, face-down, and the gold pen had been uncapped. For Tom, the thought of reading the notebook left as soon as it came; his curiosity immediately slain by his fear of being caught. The smell of brewing coffee, toast, and sautéed mushrooms slowly wafted into the bedroom, awakening Tom's stomach with a growl.

"Smells great in here! What are you making?"

"Ever hear of a full English breakfast?" Tom shook his head. "I've been hooked on them ever since I lived in the UK."

"I didn't know you lived over there."

"I did a bit of corporate legal work there after I passed the bar exam. Anyway, a full English breakfast is basically one massive plate filled with sausage, bacon, baked beans, egg, mushrooms, stewed tomatoes, and black pudding, and fried bread with toast on the side. I know it all sounds like a scattershot mess, but once you've had one there's no going back. Someone once said, 'To eat well in England you should have breakfast three times a day.' Since moving back to the States, I've tried to make as close to a full English once a week."

"So we're having all that for breakfast?"

"Well, everything but the beans, tomatoes, sausage, bacon, fried bread, and black pudding."

"What does that leave us with?"

"Eggs, mushrooms, and toast - but I make a damn good fried egg."

"It was Oscar Wilde that said, 'Only dull people are brilliant at breakfast,' so don't take too much pride in your eggs... By the way, what's black pudding?"

"Trust me, you don't want to know."

Tom watched with wonder from as Andy cooked for him. It had been years since anyone made him breakfast.

"What other bits of furniture are you selling?"

"Pretty much whatever you see except the dining table and chairs where you're sitting now."

"How come? Most of it looks practically brand new."

"A lot of it is. All I can think about when I see this stuff is my old life, and it makes me feel like none of it is actually mine. I know it's stupid and that it's only stuff, just things with no actual significance aside from what I myself project onto them, but I can't avoid feeling tied down by it all somehow. It's like that old saying, 'You don't own your possessions, your possessions own you.' I want to get rid of everything but the bare basics and try to live a simpler life with less   distractions. My car was the first thing to go. I paid off what was left and sold it to the first person to respond to the ad. I lost quite a bit of money, but selling it was something I really felt that I had to do."

"How come?"

"My wife picked it out just after I came out to her as some last-ditch effort to try to hang on to me. I didn't need a new car but she's not the type to back down. She insisted I was probably just going through a phase and that maybe getting a car would fill a void or be the change I needed."

"Let me guess - was it a sleek, mid-life crisis sports car?"

"Actually, she pushed me into buying a big luxury SUV with a huge engine. She's the one who got a little convertible."

"When's the last time you spoke to her?"

"I honestly can't remember. Even though we lived together for a while after the divorce, we didn't speak to each other. When the sale of our house went through, she moved in with her father. I couldn't get ahold of her to let her know I was moving up here to Belton so I just left a message on her answering service. Oh well."

Tom stretched his bare foot under the table to caress Andy's legs. His heart again seemed to beat harder the second their skin made contact. He wondered, *Would we be as candid with each other if we had sex last night? Hell, would I still be here at his house having breakfast?*

"You okay, Tom?" Andy looked concerned as Tom blankly stared into the kitchen directly behind Andy. Andy confusedly turned and looked over his shoulder. "Is there something wrong?"

"No, sorry. I'm just not a morning person. It takes me a little while to fully come around." *Liar.* "So how do you plan on getting around without a car?"

"I'm not sure yet. I kinda like the idea of having to walk from place-to-place but this town just isn't suited for pedestrians.

I'll probably hold off on getting a car until I absolutely have to."

The doorbell suddenly rang with a chintzy digital excerpt of 'We Wish You A Merry Christmas'. Tom looked bewildered.

"Dammit, I thought I fixed that yesterday."

Andy ran to the front window and peered out at a massive yellow pickup truck covered in aftermarket attachments, decals, and lights. Atop huge wheels with viciously rough treads, the truck towered over Tom's sedan in the driveway. Two men stood at the door, both wearing vivid NASCAR T-shirts and blue jeans. One knocked again, giggling, and shouted, "Jehovah's Witnesses!" After a quick inspection, they handed Andy some cash and carried the chair to the truck, struggling to lift the heavy wingback chair high up into the truck-bed. As they drove away, the echoing blare of the engine ripped violently through the neighborhood, setting off the alarm of a small coupe parked on the street.

Andy walked back to the dining room and ran his hand through Tom's thick auburn hair, watching with fascination as the warming mid-morning sunlight made it glow crimson.

"Tom, I hope I'm not being too forward, but I really want to see more of you."

"I'd like that too."

"This begs the question," Andy said in a ditzy voice. "Does this make you my boyfriend?"

Tom's eyes widened in alarm. "Gosh, I don't know! I've never been anyone's boyfriend before. Well, not genuinely. I mean -" Tom's mouth went dry as he restlessly shifted about in position. His loss for words amused Andy. "Sorry, I've just never been in a real relationship with another guy. Plus, I've only just met you a couple days ago."

"Hey, don't worry about it. It was a stupid thing to ask, even if I was somewhat joking. Just to be clear - I don't want you to

72

feel rushed or uncomfortable in any way. Just ignore I even said anything."

Tom felt moved. "It wasn't a stupid thing to ask. It was sweet, even if you sounded silly asking it." Andy smiled gleefully. "I want you to know that I've not felt rushed or uncomfortable at all. If anything I've just felt a bit hesitant because of how unfamiliar all of this is for me."

"What do you mean?"

"Well I really like you - and don't think I've never *really* liked someone before."

"This is all new for me too you know. I mean, I loved my wife in my own way but my relationship to her wasn't something I could fully give myself to. So much of who I am had to be separate from our relationship, but things are so different now. I know it's too early to tell anything about us - or even to say that there is an *us* - but I don't want to do anything that could ruin any future we could have together. ... I also know there's something unsettling about me being in a new place, in a new situation. I won't lie - I love the uncertainty. I dread it at times, but I really love it. All my life I've known exactly what was in store for me, and because of that, I never felt excited or enthusiastic about what lied ahead. But now, surrounded by this strange uncertainty, I feel like chance itself led me right here, in front of you right now... and I'm not about to forsake it."

They paused and looked at each other with a deep, calm intensity. Tom said, "I think the reason I seem so hesitant about all of this is because I feel something for you that I can't name or recognize - which can only be a good thing I guess. I don't know how else to say this, but if you're willing to give this a try, then I am too."

As they embraced, the doorbell rang.

"Shit - they're early," Andy hissed.

"Who's early?"

"The people buying my coffee table. They said they'd call first, but oh well. I'll only be a little while."

Just as before, Andy dashed to the front window and two men came in, handed Andy some cash, carried away the table, and drove away in a large pickup truck. With all the countless changes in the air, a large part of Tom was happy to see something even remotely familiar.

10

Susan wiped the dry, gritty sleep from her eyes and turned her head to read 11:36 AM in bright red digits on her alarm clock.

There's no way we'll make it to noon Mass.

Through the apartment's thin walls, Susan could hear the shrill sound of cartoons blaring from the television in the living room. Roberto and her father sat on the sofa fixated with the TV program and didn't notice Susan as she entered the room, disoriented by the bright light of the fluorescent bulbs overhead. The glass coffee table in front of the television was strewn with a milk carton, several cereal boxes, a used bowl, and a pile of wet paper towels surrounded by a thin pool of milk. Roberto's bowl was next to him on the sofa with his wet spoon laying to the side of it.

"Hi honey! Pour yourself a bowl and join us."

Susan did as she was told and walked to the living room, opting for the one type of cereal she knew wouldn't be teeming with sugar. She tipped the dusty remains into her bowl and poured the lukewarm milk on top, ignoring a strong compulsion to tidy the table. Never looking away from the television screen, Roberto smiled as his sister sat next to him. He seemed totally engrossed by the cartoon and Susan ate silently while bracing her bowl in case he got excited.

"You were sleeping so hard this morning that I couldn't bring myself to wake you," her father said. "We can always go to the seven o'clock mass tonight so you can take it easy until then. You deserve it honey."

"Thanks Daddy."

"And I know you like to cook for us on a Sunday morning, but Robby and I couldn't wait to eat. Sorry about that."

"It's no problem."

"You can always make us breakfast tomorrow morning. It's not like you have school anymore!" José stood and kissed Susan on the forehead as he walked to the bathroom.

"Mm-hmm," Susan said staring at the television as the cartoon program switched to a commercial break. The voice of a brash announcer yelled as the screen showed children fiercely enjoying themselves as they smashed action figures through walls of plastic blocks. It was a household custom to mute the commercials but Susan couldn't be bothered. She finished her cereal and immediately began tidying the living room, stumbling as she walked to the kitchen with a handful of soggy paper towels.

Roberto turned the television off and walked up to his sister, looking into her eyes. "You look sad Susie."

"I'm not sad, I'm just a bit tired."

"Not tired, you look sad. Is it cause we have to go to church?"

"No Robby. What gave you that idea?"

Roberto's eyes narrowed as he stared into Susan's with a look of curious suspicion as he knew full well that Susan begrudgingly went to church. There was a time when Susan truly enjoyed attending church and the different youth ministry events, but recently, church had become a very cold, dreary place for her. In the weeks following her mother's death, many people in the congregation showed their concern for the Ortega family and offered their help. However, one Sunday morning before Mass, Susan overheard a small group of women boasting about the total hours they each spent helping the Ortegas with the domestic work. Susan was so shocked and disgusted by the way they competed with each other that she locked herself in her father's car for the entirety of the services. From then on, she became cynical of the deliberate showiness that so many in the congregation displayed and found it difficult even to converse with many of the people in her parish.

Susan already had a hard time socializing with people her age from church. They piously strolled through school adorned with WWJD wristbands, purity rings, and crucifixes, but Susan and the rest of her classmates knew all about what they got up to in private. Their duplicity filled Susan with contempt. After a while, this contempt developed into a hardened indifference that Susan tried to counter by volunteering on the weekends and engaging in supplementary Bible reading. The less she felt, the harder she tried to evoke a feeling.

When Susan was seven years old, she was involved in a small fistfight with another girl at school. Her mother had to leave work to retrieve her from the principal's office. Sharon brought Susan to the back of the patrol car and opened the door for her as if she was being arrested. Sharon lifted the little girl into the car, careful not to hit her head, and slowly walked to the driver door. Susan remembered trembling in anxiety as to what her punishment would be, but as Sharon sat down, she turned back towards Susan and told her something that would forever stay with her.

"Susie, I want you to pay close attention to me because I'm only going to tell you this once as it's the most important lesson I can ever teach you: Do good even when nobody is looking. Don't do this for me, for your father, for God or for anyone else - do it for yourself. The only way we can be good people, true to ourselves, is if we try our hardest to be decent and kind *all* the time regardless of what happens around us."

Maybe it was the effect of her mother in full uniform or just the tone of unruffled seriousness in her voice, but Susan remembered her mother's words verbatim. Every time she was faced with a moral dilemma, Susan found herself recalling her mother's words and finding comfort in their simplicity. They acted as a mantra that seemed to bring Susan perspective to her own situation and helped guide her decisions, especially when dealing with others. Despite the hypocrisy and insincerity that seemed to permeate so much of her dealings with the church, Susan volunteered much of her time there because she felt it was the right thing to do.

Every Sunday, Roberto fell totally silent the second the family arrived at the chapel until they drove home. Being at church made him feel sad and confused, but he didn't have the heart or the right words to tell his father. As the Ortegas arrived and made their way through the open front doors of the church, Susan turned her head and peered into the far corner of the auditorium to where the paramedic stood at her mother's funeral. Every Sunday, Susan would mentally picture the paramedic leaning against the back wall, her reflective yellow jacket glistening in the colored light of the stained glass above the altar. This was the one ritual Susan performed at church with keenness, despite being fully aware of the futility of the act. As time passed, Susan's memory of the paramedic's face blurred and she found it difficult to remember anything other than the woman's green eyes and brown hair.

After the service, Susan and her father stood and shook hands with those around them, exchanging greetings of peace. Roberto had fallen asleep and was oblivious to the arms that wove above him, entwined in a habitual well-wishing. As Susan and her father mixed with the congregation, Susan noticed the way people changed their tone and manner as she approached them. Their heads slightly bowed in an acknowledgement of her presence, their mouths narrowed as they spoke in a tactful hush, and their eyes sent respectful half-smiles to show concern and sympathy. Irrespective of the mild distrust of some of her fellow worshippers, Susan knew that these people had a distinct regard for her and her family. This camaraderie was the one tangible aspect of the church that kept her coming back, but she knew it wasn't enough to keep her there forever.

As the Ortegas left the church, Susan again looked to the far corner and wondered what the paramedic was doing that very moment.

11

As the sun set, Tom and Andy sat side by side in canvas chairs on Andy's back porch, holding hands while looking out at the well-kept business park behind Andy's backyard.

"Sometimes when I sit out here I feel like I'm back at the house where I grew up," Andy said. "We lived on a golf course in a small suburb of Houston called Richmond. We only moved there because we needed to get a house big enough for me and my seven brothers and sisters -"

"Seven!?"

This didn't break Andy's stride; people from large families are used to being interrupted. "- yeah, seven. Anyway, the first night I moved here to Belton, I set up all my outdoor furniture and opened a bottle of wine to celebrate this new start, but I immediately felt overwhelmed with a strange homesickness."

Tom's phone rang in his pocket - Jeremy was calling.

"Do you mind if I take this?" Andy smiled and nodded. "Hi Jeremy - what's up?"

"I'm going to have to postpone our dinner date until some time when I get back."

"Sorry to hear that. Everything okay?"

"The wife wants to spend a night with me before I shoot off and leave her on her own. Plus, my son's coming down from Dallas. I forgot he'd be off work for Memorial Day."

"I had no idea you were planing on traveling alone! Of course you should spend some time with her before you leave."

"Any who, I'm also wanted calling to convince you to break away from here and go on vacation. You'll lose your mind if you stay in this heat all summer. Promise me you'll leave, okay?"

"I promise. Oh and before you go, I just wanted to let you know that I took your advice."

"Oh? Which advice?"

"About putting myself out there and being *open to the universe.* I gotta say - you were right."

"Did you get laid or something?"

Tom chuckled and said, "No no - I'm not talking about that. Do you remember lunch on Friday when I told you and Kate about this guy that I met?"

"Vaguely. I don't remember much of Friday."

"Well, I'm at his place now and I think we're officially seeing each other. Say hi, Andy."

Andy cupped his hands around his mouth and shouted, "Hello!"

"Good Lord, I tell you in passing to be open to things and now it sounds like you're part of an old married couple! ... A serious question for you, Tom: Are you happy?"

Tom stopped to think. He looked over at Andy, now bemused by a mockingbird in a tree just past the fence. Andy's head bobbed as he tried to get a better view without letting go of Tom's hand.

"I think I am."

"Then I'm happy too. Well, I need to head off and buy some meat and charcoal. I look forward to seeing you and meeting your new fellow when I get back. Take care!"

"Have fun Jeremy."

Tom hung up the phone and turned to Andy, "Sorry about that."

"Don't apologize! It must be nice to have a friend like that. Is he gay?"

"No, but at times I think he wishes he was just for some perceived cultural uniqueness. Why do you ask?"

"From what I heard coming through the phone, he sounds really camp."

"He is camp, but he's definitely not gay. He has either slept with or at least tried to sleep with half the female staff at work."

"Sounds like *such* a great guy..." Andy playfully rolled his eyes as he stood and stretched his arms.

"He really is once you get to know him. Plus he's one of the only male members of staff that treats me like a human being instead of the office queer."

"People at work actually treat you differently?"

"You have to realize that you're not in Houston any more. The further you get away from a big city - especially in the South - the more traditionalist and conservative people are. Women are more likely to be accepting but there's still this bullshit machismo culture here that keeps the men so intolerant. It really doesn't help that we're so close to the Army base... Anyway,, I was supposed to meet up with Jeremy for a meal tomorrow night but that fell through."

"So you're free tomorrow night then?" Andy winked and smirked at Tom.

"Well I guess so."

"What about tonight? Did you have any plans?"

Tom thought, *We're not moving too fast, are we?*

Andy put his hand on Tom's shoulder. "Sorry, I don't mean to be so presumptuous. If you've got plans then I understand."

"No. You're not being presumptuous at all. Nothing would make me happier than spending the rest of the evening with you. And yes, I'm free tomorrow night too."

Andy beamed with elation.

Tom said, "You know, you look like a kid when you get excited."

"I know, I know. And you - when you're deep in thought you look like my dad when he's frustrated."

"Is that supposed to make me feel good? Plus, what does it say about you if you're in a romantic relationship with someone that looked like your father?"

Andy's smile turned to a pained grimace. "Actually I don't really want to think about this any further." He peered away for a few seconds then sat back down next to Tom. He looked into Tom's eyes and any previous sense of embarrassment faded from his face. "I do like the sound of this 'romantic relationship' stuff though. Tell me more about it."

With a teacher's wizened gaze, Tom said, "Well, Andy, when a mommy and a daddy love each other *very* much - "

"You're such a smart ass! Here I am trying to be sweet and you're making a joke out of it!"

"Sorry. I'm a bit new to this relationship stuff."

Andy leaned down to Tom and kissed him on the forehead. "I'm starving. What do you say we heat up some of your sister's food?"

"Oh, dear god no. It was horrible yesterday - I don't know what could possibly make you think it's going to be any good today. Going to my sister's place really shouldn't count as our first date, so why don't we go out tonight?"

"Sure! Where to?"

"How does sushi sound?"

"Great! Can we walk there?"

"Well, it's about a mile each way."

"Then what are we waiting for? If I'm already this hungry, I'll be ravenous by the time we finally get there!"

As they walked through downtown Belton, Tom looked at his surroundings with a warm familiarity he hadn't felt in years. The streetlights switched on as Tom and Andy strolled past the riverbank and the water's sweet, metallic smell triggered Tom's memory of days in town with his father.

Tom said, "Dad and I used to walk over this river crossing at least once a month on our way to the tennis courts, but I've nearly forgotten what it looked like. So much of it has changed over the years, but all the smells and sounds are the same."

A gentle gust blew along the stream, lightly wafting fireflies as they hovered just above the water's surface; their faint glow reflected off the slowly flowing water like flickering tea light candles. Tom briefly thought about all the places in the world he could be visiting on vacation, then quickly banished the thought from his head. He plucked a long strand of dry tawny grass jutting out of a crack in the concrete and twirled it between his fingers. Andy took one as well and stuck it in the side of his mouth before dancing an exaggerated jig on the sidewalk.

"You really are a big kid, Andy."

"Which makes you a pervert, Tom."

Andy reached for Tom's hand - but Tom quickly pulled away as if by instinct. Andy looked insulted. "What's the matter?"

"Sorry. It's nothing personal, but I don't want to be a spectacle."

"What do you mean?"

"This is a small town and seeing two gay men actually *being* gay is only going to agitate them."

"So what? Aren't you proud of who you are?"

"Of course I am, but for me this isn't a matter of pride. I know what the people are like around here. They're not very tolerant of people like us and I don't feel like being anyone's target. All I want is to live and enjoy my life on my own terms without any unnecessary grief."

"Fair enough." As they walked off, Andy sneakily pinched Tom's backside eliciting a scornful scowl from Tom that quickly turned into a smile.

Walking through the restaurant doors, Andy flinched at the

sudden high flames that burst off the surface of a hibachi grill. All the dining tables and places at the hibachis were occupied or booked, so Tom and Andy sat at the sushi bar. Parched from the walk, they ordered two large lagers which they guzzled down in no time. Tom immediately ordered more beer along with two large flasks of sake for the meal.

"So what's good here?" Andy asked as he hopped onto a padded stool.

"Everything really. If I'm sat at the bar, I usually ask the sushi chefs to make whatever they want and I've never been disappointed. They always serve up something insanely elaborate and tend to charge me for the basic, cheaper dishes. But only order that way if you're feeling adventurous. You never really know what you'll get."

"Sounds great."

Tom and Andy chatted and joked with the chefs as they fashioned colorful plates of abstract expressionist sushi. More sake was ordered.

"Tom," Andy asked, "do you enjoy what you do?"

"Huh?"

"Do you enjoy teaching?"

"Oh... I guess so. It's been difficult the past few years with all the budget cuts. The pay's never been fantastic, and on top of cutting loads of programs, they've frozen all the salaries and have dumbed-down the curriculum to mold to the standardized tests. I do my best to work all the good books and poetry into the first couple months of the school year before everyone gets carried away with the big exams. Still, it's hard to get the kids to care. I've never seen a more distracted group of students than I have this last year, but I'm honestly not surprised. Life seems to be nothing but distractions these days and I'm amazed when any of my students decide to turn something in. ... I think it's easy to get upset with where education seems to be headed, especially if you're inside the system, but once you get past all the tedious protocols and bullshit bureaucratic red tape, it's alright. You don't stick around as a teacher unless it's something you really want to do. Why do you ask?"

"Well, my wife used to be a teacher. She quit in 2004, mostly because of all the No Child Left Behind bullshit."

"What did she teach?"

"Chemistry. She was a total science geek when I met her and nothing ever changed. She works in pharmaceuticals now. ... God, I really should stop talking about her. I bet she's the last thing you want to hear about."

"I don't mind."

"You're just saying that. Nobody wants to hear someone go on and on about their ex."

"Honestly, it's not a big deal. The only reason I don't mention my exes is because I don't have any. If anything, I'm intrigued by it all."

Andy humbly smiled at Tom and discreetly stroked his knee under the bar, carefully trying not to overstep Tom's personal boundaries on privacy. After green tea ice cream and even more sake for dessert, they paid the bill and headed home. The night breeze gently swayed the trees and tall grass lining the road as Tom and Andy staggered along Main Street. Mere blocks away from Andy's house, they stood at an intersection waiting for the pedestrian signal to change and as a black family sedan passed, Andy stuck his thumb out, playfully hitching for a ride. Tom leapt over and grabbed Andy's hand, lowering it while signaling the driver to keep going. Andy drunkenly threw his arm around Tom and squeezed him just as a small red coupe with a large exhaust pipe growled past. A man with short, cropped hair and wrap-around sunglasses leaned out of the passenger window and shouted, "Fucking faggots!"

Veins bulged in Andy's neck as he screamed with every ounce

of his being, "YOU COWARD!"

The car's tires screeched as it braked and squealed as it spun around and quickly raced back towards them, mounting the pavement and stopping a few yards in front of Tom and Andy. The man with the sunglasses stepped out of the passenger door and another man with a similar buzz-cut and baggy clothes followed closely behind.

"The fuck did you call me?!"

"I called you a coward."

"And why the fuck would you do something stupid like that?"

Andy pointed and said, "Because you cowardly shouted something at me as you drove away. I'm pretty sure doing that sort of thing is what defines a coward."

The man walked up to Andy and pushed him in the chest. "Would a coward come back to kick your queer ass?"

"After you've been called out, what does it matter? I'll tell you your options..."

The man in sunglasses laughed as Andy clumsily pulled a pen out
of his pocket. "Ha! This should be good, Jeff."

Andy quickly scribbled something on the inside of his right hand and returned the pen to his pocket. "Right - you have two options here. One, you can stay and fight after using a homophobic slur, which would essentially be committing a hate-crime. That's a federal offense with a long prison sentence *and* a fine on top of that. I've written down your license plate number and I'd have no problem finding the rest of your information, *Jeff*. It's one of the perks of being a lawyer. Your other option would be to leave now and maintain whatever masculine dignity you think you still have. If you're smart, you'd take this fucking faggot's professional advice and go with the latter."

The driver grabbed his partner by the arm and whispered

something in his ear. The man in the sunglasses grunted in anger and shot Andy a look of hatred as he prowled back towards the car. The tires screamed as they skidded off the curb while a middle finger was held out of the passenger window.

Tom looked over and saw Andy's body shaking with adrenaline. He put his arm around Andy's shoulder and they swiftly walked back home. As soon as they walked in the front door, they kissed wildly. A rush of pleasure hit Andy and he moaned with surprised rapture as Tom's hands slid up his shirt and grabbed his ribs. Andy squeezed Tom towards him and felt Tom's erection on his stomach through their clothes. Andy took off his shirt and moved his hands down Tom's sides and around to rest in his back pockets. Despite the adrenaline in their system, they were both still slightly drunk and sleepily full of food. Their graceless fumbles on the sofa gradually grew more clumsy and uninhibited while they kissed and fondled each other's bodies. As Tom's shirt came off he leaned forward to kiss Andy but lost his balance and fell towards him, bashing their lips together. Both winced in pain and laughed as they checked for any broken skin.

"Please tell me you'll keep this sofa," Tom pleaded.

"Why?"

"I've grown fond of it over these last couple days."

"Sorry, but I really don't like it. It's ugly and we seem to keep hurting ourselves on here, so it's obviously unlucky."

Tom grabbed Andy by his bare left nipple and twisted it just hard enough to evoke a reaction. "Too bad. Promise me you'll keep it!"

"Ow! Okay! Okay!"

Tom twisted a little harder. "Now promise me you'll keep the table and chairs on the back porch!"

"No! They're still for sale online!" Andy winced, totally at

Tom's mercy.

"Then I'll buy them from you so I can leave them here!" He released Andy and covered his own chest to avoid the same treatment. "How much?"

Andy touched his now sensitive nipple. "Oh I'm sure I can think of a price." He stood from the sofa and held his hand out to Tom while trying to mask a yawn. Hand-in-hand, Tom sleepily followed Andy to the bedroom. Tom stopped in the doorway as they entered the bedroom and watched Andy as he walked over to his nightstand. Andy turned on the bedside lamp and placed his wristwatch next to the notebook. He slowly walked back to Tom, admiring his bare chest in the dim, shadowy light.

"Andy, please undress me."

Andy nodded; his expression didn't change. With their eyes locked in gaze, Andy loosened Tom's belt. He unfastened the top button on Tom's shorts and then slowly opened the zipper, then knelt and put his hands on Tom's hips, gently lowering his shorts to the ground. Tom was very visibly erect and Andy could easily see the outline through the briefs.

"Those too."

Andy looked into Tom's eyes and slowly lowered the briefs to the floor, then Andy took a step back and put his hand to his chin as he gazed at Tom's nude body.

"You're beautiful, Tom." Without touching him, Andy's gaze returned to Tom's eyes. "Could you now undress me, please?"

"It would be my pleasure."

Tom mirrored Andy's movements perfectly. Belt, shorts, briefs - all removed with the same patient, considerate, gentle movements. They stood in front of each other, their hands slowly gliding over the other's naked body.

This is all we are, no room for pretension.

Instinctively they began to make the encounter more physical, but both Tom and Andy lacked the energy to go very far. They slowly, sleepily explored each other's bodies as they kissed, laughing at their own bumbling strokes and caresses. The periodic tastes and aromas of the other only briefly broke the spell of slumber and within minutes, they slid beneath the sheets in willing defeat and spooned each other affectionately before falling asleep in each others' arms.

12

At 8:53, the Ortegas ate alone in the indoor playground area of a fast food restaurant. Roberto left the unwrapped toy from his kid's meal next to a few thin scattered french fries and a mound of ketchup as he climbed through plastic tunnels, occasionally peering down at Susan and their father through Perspex peepholes. Roberto stopped enjoying these play areas months ago after kneeling in another child's urine at the top of a spiral slide, but his father still used the promise of chicken nuggets to arouse enthusiasm for church.

Susan sat with her head leaned against a large pane glass window branded by bold, colorful characters advertising a seasonal sandwich. Her expression erratically twisted as she reflected on the day's sermon given by the assistant pastor. He began by lecturing about the need to fully give oneself to God and congregation, but by the end of the discourse he focused on the effect of worship on personal wealth. He shouted, 'Give yourself to God, and God will reward you!' so many times, Susan stopped counting. Susan was used to his empty rhetoric and usually tuned out when he spoke, but there was something about his tone that night at Mass that particularly unsettled Susan.

"You ok, Susie?"

"Yeah Dad. Just thinking about church."

"It was a good sermon today - wasn't it?"

"Yeah Dad."

"I love Brother Jones' fiery sermons. They're always so much more memorable than those wishy-washy, love-thy-neighbor snore-fests Pastor Simmons gives."

Susan bit the inside of her lip to keep quiet.

On the drive home, Susan saw two men walking on the sidewalk along Main Street. As the car approached, one of them stuck his thumb out like a hitchhiker while the other embarrassingly waved them on. Susan's father turned his head to see them and he furrowed his brow as he muttered, "Stupid drunks." Though José wasn't able to make out the mens' faces, Susan could clearly see that the man waving was her former teacher Mr. Woodbine, but she said nothing. Susan found out Tom was gay the night her family moved into the apartment complex where he lived. Before then, she occasionally overheard some of the other students and teachers share rumors and jokes about him behind his back, but she never put any credence to their remarks. She could never understand why so many people seemed to care so much about an aspect of another person's life that would never personally affect them. Ever since the first day in Tom's class, Susan immediately sensed an honesty and kindness in him and felt closer to him than anyone else at school.

The night Susan and her family moved into the apartment complex, Susan felt stricken by an unfamiliar anxiety. Deep down she knew their move was necessary, but as she sat in the middle of her new room, looking at all her boxed possessions in their new surroundings, Susan was overwhelmed by a nagging urge to leave. Her father laid unconscious on the sofa next to a bottle of rum and Roberto had long since fallen asleep, so in her pajamas and plush house slippers, Susan tiptoed out the front door unnoticed and quietly shut the door behind her. Just as she felt the doorknob click shut, Susan realized she was locked outside without a key and a wave of self-loathing struck her. Frustrated but powerless to her compulsion to leave, Susan silently walked down the second-floor corridor past several of her new neighbors, ducking as she passed their windows. To Susan, the muffled laughter of late night TV talk shows flickering behind blinds and curtains felt like a mocking fanfare. As she neared the end of the passage, Susan heard two men talking in the parking lot as one climbed into his small jeep. She ducked down behind a pillar to try to listen in on their conversation, but the men spoke too quietly. As she poked her head around the pillar for a better look, Susan's eyes widened as she watched the men sensually kiss.

Susan had never seen two men kissing and was stunned by the sight. She had a gay aunt on her mother's side in Dallas but the Ortegas rarely saw her or her partner. There was never any mention of homosexuality in their house just as there was never any mention of her father's time spent in Kuwait during the Desert Storm campaign. The two topics were always a taboo that would only make Susan's parents clam up and change the subject when mentioned.

As the jeep drove away, the man in the parking lot walked back to his apartment and briefly looked in the direction of Susan's hiding spot. She sneakily caught a quick glimpse of his face and immediately recognized he was her English teacher, Mr. Woodbine. After a few moments of trying to make sense of the situation, Susan realized that she honestly didn't know how to feel. She knew that people around her were uncomfortable regarding any gay issues and that the kids around her only used the word 'gay' to describe anything they disliked. At church, homosexuality was openly chastised and condemned as a sin. Susan remembered her pastor describing it as an act that inhibited those practicing it from 'inheriting God's Kingdom' - *whatever that means*. But still, Susan could not see the courteous interaction between Mr. Woodbine and his *friend* as something inherently wrong. Susan watched Tom as he walked across to the adjacent apartment block to his apartment, waiting until he closed his door before leaving her hiding spot. A mist began to form in the night air just above the rooflines of the apartment buildings as she walked down the nearest steps and around the perimeter of the complex. After a complete circuit of the premises in the chilly November air, Susan sat down on one of the benches in the communal garden and began thinking about her father on the sofa.

She thought, *If Dad was drunk enough to pass out with his shoes and jacket still on, how crazy will he go if he found out I snuck out at night? He'll probably yell and scream and the whole neighborhood will hate him after only the first night. Plus, Robby would be so confused at all the noise he'd probably start crying right away.*

After ten minutes of shivering on the bench, Susan realized her only other option was to knock on Mr. Woodbine's door and hope he'd let her in. Through the half-shut mini-blinds, she could see the light of a small lamp in Tom's living room and she heard music quietly playing as she neared the door. Susan gently knocked on the door just quietly enough for it to go unnoticed by the neighbors. Seconds later, the music stopped and Susan could hear footsteps near the door.

Oh shit.

Tom opened the door and his eyes widened in confusion.

"Susan? What are you doing here?"

"Hi Mr. Woodbine. I just moved in across from you and locked myself out. Can I come in?"

"Is nobody home at your apartment?"

"Well, my dad's there but he's passed out on the sofa. Can I please come in?"

Tom poked his head out and surveyed the apartment complex. "Did anyone see you come over here?"

"I don't think so."

As he reached his arm out around her and pulled her inside, he could feel she was shaking. "Would you like something hot to drink?"

"Mmm-hmm."

"Do you like tea?"

"Sure."

The room fell silent as the kettle slowly heated. Tom knew Susan's situation regarding her mother's death and had heard rumors that her father wasn't taking the loss very well.

"I have green tea and chamomile," Tom said. "Which would you like?"

"What are they like?"

"Chamomile tea is light and floral while green tea is crisp and slightly bitter."

"Chamomile, please."

The tea brewed and Tom brought the cups and saucers into the living room on a small plastic tray.

"What music were you listening to?"

"Ever hear of a singer called Kate Bush?"

"No. Is she on the radio?"

"Not exactly. Do you want me to put it back on?"

"Please."

He turned the stereo back on and restarted the song - 'This Woman's Work'.

"I really like her voice." Susan thought the singer's voice sounded how the tea tasted.

"She has an incredible voice. She used to get *really* crazy on some of her earlier songs, but this is a really gentle one."

"But her voice sounds so strong."

"She's beyond strong. She's written, recorded, produced, and performed so much of her own music, unlike a lot of the junk on the radio. I think the album she did before this one is possibly the best album of the last century."

"Wow! Can you put it on next?"

Tom turned to Susan with a concerned look. "How long were you planning on being here?"

"I don't know. If I go back now Daddy's gonna make a big deal about it. He- He's had a bit to drink and I don't want to bother him until it wears off."

Tom didn't know how to respond.

"How about this," Susan said. "I could stay until really early in the morning and then act like I woke up early and locked myself out. My dad won't be so worried or upset that I have to wake him up."

"You're asking to stay the night?!" Tom thought - *I really shouldn't even be considering this. What if the neighbors found out? What if the school found out?*

"I'm sorry I bothered you Mr. Woodbine. I don't know what I was thinking. I'm so stupid sometimes."

"No - no you're not! You're one of the smartest kids I've ever had in my classroom, and I'm not talking grades here: You're smarter and more experienced than the rest of the kids in your class will probably ever be. For most of them, life is just handed to them bit-by-bit. Do you know what I'm trying to say?" She nodded her head. "Look, I can bring some blankets and pillows out here for you on the sofa. I'll wake up at 6 so we can make sure you're up really early. Okay?"

"Thanks Mr. Woodbine! ... Can we finish listening to the music first?"

"Sure. Do you like it?"

"I love it!"

Tom wished Susan goodnight as the album finished and shut off the lights as he walked to his room. Sliding underneath his covers, Tom thought, *How did she know which apartment was mine? Her's is on the other side of the complex and there were loads of neighbors around her that are still awake...but she came all the way over here. Oh fuck, she must have seen me with David - which means she must have seen us kissing!*

Tom had a hard time falling asleep and could only catch a

96

couple hours of sleep before having to get up and send Susan on her way. He never heard anything from Susan about any repercussions from that night and assumed the best.

The next weekend, the apartment complex held a residents' barbecue that the landlords catered. It was nothing special but almost all of the tenants were present. Susan spent the day with her father meeting all of her new neighbors while trying to keep an eye on Roberto. He had a fascination with open fires and the occasional flash of white smoke let her know he was putting more leaves on the barbecue. Later in the evening, Susan's father started talking to another teacher from her school - Stephen Kim. Susan only caught the end of the conversation, but she heard him joke about how he wished all gay people could be sent off to an island and then exterminated. The determined hatred in his face as he joked made Susan feel disgusted. Tom sat nearby talking to some of the other neighbors, but he too could hear Stephen's joke. Susan watched Tom as he bit his lip, trying his hardest not to react or even acknowledge such a cruel thought. Seeing the painful effect of those words, Susan realized that such a standpoint could only be wrong, regardless of any religious or moral backing.

When Susan and her family arrived home from the fast food restaurant, she decided she would go back to church the following day for the Memorial Day services. Something about this last sermon troubled her and she felt a strong need to speak with the head pastor.

13

Susan awoke at 7:00 AM just like she would have done on a normal school day. She took her time to shower and prepare herself before cooking a big skillet of scrambled eggs with fried potatoes and chorizo for the family. José had planned to take his children out for a day at the lake to play on the beach and on the paddle-boats. He was upset when Susan said she'd rather go to church, but he didn't try to convince her otherwise.

Susan was astonished by the amount of decorations lining the streets as she drove through town to church. She had forgotten how seriously the military community here took Memorial Day and all the other patriotic holidays. At church, Pastor Simmons allotted most of his sermon time for silent reflection on the dead and for the soldiers fighting in different offensives around the world. On one of the many moments of silence, Susan tried to think about what the memorial of the fallen soldiers meant to her, but she truly couldn't. All the stock lines she was taught by her parents and teachers growing up came to mind, but none of it actually meant anything to her.

She thought, *What's the point of being so reflective on the past deaths of soldiers when we're only going to send more out to die?*

Susan knew there were a couple people from school who joined the Army and recently died in Iraq and Afghanistan. She shared an art class with a boy named Jon who graduated a semester early to join the Army from the Junior ROTC program. She remembered him ranting about job security and how much spare money he'd have since the Army paid all his living expenses on base. For Jon, enlisting seemed like a no-brainer since he couldn't see himself spending any more time in school. One day, she confronted him about where he stood on the conflicts in Iraq and Afghanistan and if he could justify fighting there, and his answer was seemingly simple.

"I'll fight where I'm told to fight."

"Do you feel like you'll be protecting your country?"

"Of course I do!" He looked at Susan as if she was an idiot.

"But you'd be on the other side of the planet fighting people who are only trying to protect their way of life from outsiders who invaded on false pretenses. Plus, you just said you'd be fighting because it's your job. Wouldn't that just make you an armed bully with a salary?"

He replied with a few choice profanities and accused Susan of being a liberal traitor of her country. Susan could only take so much of his verbal abuse before she walked away from the conversation, realizing there was no point in any further discussion. A year later, Susan saw a local news bulletin that made her feel sick to her stomach. The reporter announced the death of Jon and seven other soldiers in Afghanistan in a friendly fire incident.

She thought - *What is there to reflect on?*

Susan waited for the audience to disperse a half-hour after the services finished before approaching Pastor Simmons, a short, slender man well into his seventies, wearing a modest black suit with subtle pinstripes. She stared at the slight curve in his back as he bent down to gather his books from inside the podium on stage.

"Pastor Simmons - do you have some time to talk?"

"For you Susan, of course I do. What's up?"

"I have a few personal issues I need to get off my chest and I just need someone to listen."

The pastor looked at her with concern. "Susan, would you be

okay with Brother Jones sitting in with us? He's undergoing some ministerial training and needs to do a bit of observation."

"Um, I guess that's okay." Susan wasn't pleased, but the need to talk far outweighed her apprehension. They walked back into a private room and Brother Jones joined them a few moments later. He wore a glossy plaid three-button suit with shoulder-pads and a loud multicolored tie in a large knot. He sat down next to Pastor Simmons with a loud exhale as his large frame fell into the seat.

Pastor Simmons clasped his hands and softly said, "So Susan, what do you want to talk about?"

"Well, it's not easy for me to talk about this, but it's like I don't actually *feel* anything when I'm at church anymore. And when I try to remember when I did feel something - I can't. It's not like I'm not doing anything bad in my personal life that could blemish my conscience, so I don't know what it could be that's making me feel so indifferent."

"Susie," Brother Jones said, "do you pray?"

"I've always prayed since I was a little girl and still do."

"Well what does God tell you?"

"What does God tell me? He's never told me anything. I've always told him everything but I don't hear back, nor do I expect to."

"You're just not listening hard enough, Susie."

"That's ridiculous!" Susan felt hurt by this claim. "What does God tell *you*, Brother Jones?"

"He tells me all sorts of things. When I pray for an answer to a question, He gives me little hints along the way to guide me."

"Couldn't that just be reasoning?"

Pastor Simmons said, "Brother Jones, I believe Susan came here to talk, not be lectured to. Isn't that right Susan?... Okay then. So you say you feel indifferent. What is it that you feel indifferent towards?"

"Here lately - everything really. You know how involved I am in the congregation. I love so many of the people here and feel so thankful and blessed that they would help us out in our time of need. But I find that they've been the only thing keeping me coming back to church, and now even that appeal is starting to fade."

"Okay. Susan I know this is a difficult question, but it's one I feel I need to ask: How have things been at home since your mother died?"

"Well, I can't say things have been easy. Between school, coming here for volunteer work, and making sure that Dad and Roberto are okay I find myself tired all the time - but it's a good 'tired'. My family is what matters to me the most."

Once again Brother Jones cut in. "Were you sad when your mother died?"

Pastor Simmons shot Jones a look of scorn.

"Of course I was sad! How could I not be sad?"

He smugly crossed his arms. "Well you know where you can turn for help right? The Bible. Do you read it much?"

Susan paused and collected herself before answering. "That was obviously the first place I turned to when my mother died. Since then, I've read it cover-to-cover three times. I started reading it again last month and got up to Deuteronomy before I couldn't take any more."

"You couldn't take any more?!"

"No I couldn't - it's all such a mess! The only part that gave me any comfort was the story of Jesus, but once he ascended to heaven, all the unconditional, nonjudgemental love he preached was forgotten. Then Armageddon comes. The end."

"You're bordering on blasphemy young lady! How dare you talk about His Word that way!"

Pastor Simmons leapt from his chair. "BROTHER JONES! I think you've done enough observation for today. I suggest you leave and join your family in the lobby."

"But I-"

The look on Pastor Simmons' face showed he meant business. Brother Jones gathered his briefcase and his ornately gilded Bible and as he stormed out of the room, Susan could feel his heavy stomps through the legs of her chair.

Pastor Simmons waited until the footsteps seemed out of earshot. "I'm really sorry about that Susan. His method of helping needs, well, help. I've been trying to work with him on it."

"It's okay."

"I think I know what you're trying to say about the Bible though."

"You do?"

"To be frank, the Bible isn't the best manual for modern life. I know I'm not supposed to say that, but it's the truth. However, in the Bible are all the basics - love, respect, charity, devotion. Even if you take all the genealogy, doctrine, and all the crazy Old Testament stuff out of the book, the main teachings are still about the humble respect of fellow man. When you honor and respect those around you, you're respecting yourself and your own moral code."

"But I do that on my own anyway. I don't see why I need the Bible to tell me to do something that makes logical sense."

Pastor Simmons sat back in his chair and looked at Susan contemplatively. "You know, you're something else."

"What do you mean?"

"Well, most of the people I've come across in this and other congregations just sit back and accept God, Christianity, and the whole lot exactly as it's told to them. They don't seem to question any of it - not to me at least - and it becomes an unexceptional part of their lives. I truly believe that the only way to true personal faith is through doubt. Only through questioning your beliefs can you actually understand why you believe what you believe. When you know why, it becomes real and more rewarding."

"What about those people that don't need to question their beliefs?"

"You know, I used to think they were the lucky ones. People like you and me have to yearn and struggle our way through life because we're more sensitive to the rise and fall of it all. For us, just muttering some scripted words of a prayer or throwing our hands up in a showy display just isn't going to cut it."

"But I wish it would."

"I know. ... Susan, you may never find out what it is that makes you feel this indifference. I know that's not very reassuring, but it's the honest truth. Right now you're at a crossroads in your life which could be what's making you feel anxious. You've just finished school and now you've got the whole world at your feet. I know you've stepped up in the last few months and taken on loads of responsibility with your family since your mother passed away. I know people twice your age who've collapsed under half the pressure you're under now. You're a sharp, insightful young woman with a big heart. I know times are hard now but I'm more than optimistic that things will turn out okay."

"Thanks Pastor Simmons."

"You're welcome. And please - call me Scott. ... Susan, can you keep a secret? ... I don't want everyone to know, but I'll be retiring at the end of the year and it looks like the chapel board will be taking on Brother Jones as my replacement. Underneath all the glitz and showmanship, he really is a good man and a good leader - but he's still learning to be a shepherd. Do you know what I'm trying to say?"

"I think so. One of the matters I wanted to bring up with you was his sermon from last night. All that talk of money and personal gain really upset me. What I was heard Brother Jones say conflicted with everything else I've ever heard in this church, and my conscience was telling me it was wrong."

"I know what you mean, but attendance rises when Brother Jones speaks and the congregation really seems to enjoy his sermons - and don't think the chapel board hasn't noticed. Since those new *megachurches* opened in Killeen and Temple a few years ago, our audience numbers and those of several other small local churches have dropped severely. It's happening just like the way the superstores have shut down so many small businesses by drawing away their customers. There's so much demand for their elaborate services that the megachurches hold three sermons every Sunday and several more throughout the week - all of which are filled to capacity. Some of them have credit unions, coffee shops, and restaurants inside the church to keep their parishioners and their money in one place. We'll never be able to provide all these extra perks and spectacles purely because we don't have anywhere near the amount of money they've got, but Brother Jones brings a certain flair for performance that the chapel board sees as their only way to stay afloat.

"The world's changed over the last couple generations and all the businesses, governments, schools, and churches are trying to keep up and meet or create demand. People these days want to hear how the Bible can be applied to today's more tangible issues and don't care as much about the parables and metaphors. Personally, I disagree with changing our approach to comply with the times. The message in the Bible is the same and has been the same throughout history. I believe this selective, materialistic faith system is wrong, but I'm in a small minority that's only getting smaller as time passes. The truth is, I'm retiring is because I'm not well and haven't been well for quite some time. I initially took on an assistant because I just don't have the energy for several long sermons a week anymore."

"Will you still attend services here once you've stepped down."

"Probably - unless Jones takes his shtick any further and puts a cash machine in the lobby. Then you and I can go look elsewhere!"

"Sounds like a deal."

She shook his hand and slowly walked with him out of the room. As Susan entered her car, she watched as Brother Jones chased one of his younger sons around the parking lot, shouting for him to get in the car. Susan couldn't help but laugh.

The Memorial Day parade blocked off most of Susan's regular route home so she took a detour that circled downtown Belton. After rolling her windows down to hear the blares of the high school marching band and its explosive drum-line from a few blocks away, she decided to park her car and enjoy the festivities. Hundreds of people and nearly as many Texan and American flags lined the street near the courthouse as the last of the marching band strolled past playing 'America the Beautiful'. As Susan walked through the crowd, she noticed many people turn towards her, likely recognizing her from the news. A small regiment of soldiers marched closely behind the band, carrying massive flags, and as the troops reached the stage, the audience fell totally silent. The atmosphere of the procession promptly reminded Susan of her graduation ceremony; even the stage seemed to be the same one used at the convention center.

After the national anthem and a short prayer by a clergyman in a long black robe, the local congressman approached the podium and adeptly addressed the spectators.

"Traditionally, Memorial Day has been a day where we as Americans reflect back on those we've lost in war. Even today there are many of our loved ones who are bravely serving in lands across the world. But let us never forget our loved ones who were so needlessly lost here at home - those killed in the 2009 shooting in Fort Hood, the Waco siege in '93, and all the innocents we lost in the massacre at Luby's in '91. This day is for honoring their memories. I'd like to invite you all to join me in a minute of silent reflection."

Susan closed her eyes and immediately began thinking about the night her mother died. She remembered the ambulance and walking down the hallway, holding the paramedic's hand tightly. She remembered Roberto's face as he played with one of the nurses. The way the waiting room smelled. The doctors huddled around her father. The sound her hand made against her father's face.

Susan thought, *I wonder if she watched my graduation. It didn't feel like she was watching. Mom, if you were watching, should it have felt like you were watching? If the shooting never happened and you were still alive, what would you have said to me once I found you in the audience? Would you be crying tears of happiness? What would I have said to you? Oh God, there are so many things I wish I would have said to you. I -*

"Thank you," the congressman said, breaking the silence.

The light stung Susan's eyes as she opened them. As she came around, she realized she had been crying and several people around her were staring intently. As the next speaker walked on stage and shook the congressman's hand, Susan quickly retreated through the crowd towards her car, stepping on several pairs of toes on the way. She drove straight home to an empty house, arriving shortly before three.

Dad and Roberto must still be at the lake, she thought.

Susan walked to her room and looked at her red eyes and clammy face in the mirror, frowning at a face that looked far too old for its age. She shut the door, closed the blinds, and got into bed, laying there for the next half hour trying to sleep, but sleep wouldn't come.

14

"Good morning, gorgeous."

Tom's eyes opened and his head immediately ached. "I feel like death."

"It's nice to see you too."

Tom lifted the blanket to look upon Andy's prone, naked body then snaked his head further under the covers to tickled Andy, making him writhe and scream in protest.

"I'll wet the bed if you don't stop! Seriously!"

Tom winked as he surfaced. "Sorry, I just wanted to see how ticklish you were. Been up long?"

"Not really. I got up a few minutes ago to take some painkillers. I didn't think the sake would hit me so hard, but my head is throbbing."

"Mine too. Where do you keep your pills?"

"I've left them out on the countertop for you. The glasses are above the toaster."

The soft grey light of the overcast morning sky softened the blow of waking life for Tom as he walked to the kitchen in the nude. Andy whistled a catcall as Tom reached the door, but Tom just shook his head and kept walking. His mind was still full of the lingering senses of the night before. Coming through strongest was Andy's uniquely salty-sweet flavor and aroma, somehow reminiscent of honey and cloves, that seemed embedded in Tom's nostrils and the pores of his skin. The mere thought of Andy's naked body in bed began to arouse Tom as he swallowed the tablets. Tom began to walk back towards the bedroom but stopped as he saw Andy stood leaning against the large glass doors to the backyard.

"I wanted to see you... I mean, I wanted to watch you move around naturally and just *be*. ... Sorry, I know that sounds creepy, but I wanted to see your bare legs in step, your body pivot around corners, your soft privates hang - though in this state, it looks like I won't be able to see the latter."

Tom blushed as he looked over Andy's bare body with serene contentment. Even in low light, Andy still had a glow about him like a marble sculpture on exhibition. Tom walked to Andy, took his hand, and they went back into Andy's room to make love with clumsy, sweet abandon. Every movement was performed with watchful consideration and as they each climaxed, they looked into each other's eyes without any sense of bashfulness. Afterwards they laughingly collapsed in a heap on the bed and snuggled close, falling back to sleep.

Tom woke again in the early afternoon with the sun warmly streaming in through the gauzy ivory curtains. He could hear the distant chatter of a group of people outside along the street. Andy sat cross-legged at the foot of the bed wearing only a pair of jogging shorts.

"Afternoon, Tom."

"Is it really?"

"Just barely. There are loads of people walking past into town. I'm guessing it has something to do with the parade."

"I totally forgot about it. What time is everything supposed to start?"

"We've got another hour or so before everything kicks off. I'd like to watch it if that's okay with you."

"Sure."

"My head's still killing me, but I think a strong cup of coffee will sort me out."

"Let's get moving then."

They showered and dressed quickly. Tom borrowed another

shirt and a pair of shorts from Andy's closet.

"This is getting ridiculous. I'd like to wear my own clothes some time this week. Why don't we have dinner at my place tonight and sleep there?"

"I'd really like that."

Any hint of the morning's cloud cover had been burnt away by the intense afternoon sun and as Tom and Andy opened the front door, the sounds of masses of people filled their ears and the smell of barbecue made their mouths water. They walked along the red, white, and blue decorative haze on Main Street into the festive revelry and stopped to buy coffee and hot dogs from a vendor. As the high school drum-line began its procession through the town with a mobile rendition of 'Battle Hymn of the Republic', the sudden crash of cymbals startled Tom, nearly making him drop his hot dog mid-bite. The crack of the kevlar-skinned snare drums loudly shot through the streets and ricocheted off the buildings. The brass section blazed through the air while the woodwinds cooly reigned them in. Most of the crowd saluted the marching band and color guard as they steadily trooped past along the thoroughfare.

"God, I really need the bathroom," Andy said. "Is there one around here?"

"No idea what'll be open. Let's have a wander."

They found a seemingly deserted convenience store nearby. Andy walked immediately to the bathroom while Tom waited by the newsstand. He flicked through a local paper with a special honorary section on residents lost in war. Directly underneath it was an article on the Fort Hood and Luby's massacres written by a local politician who lost both his parents in the latter. Andy bought a bottle of water and a small pack of extra-strength migraine pills and they then rejoined the crowd just as the band finished its march through the town. During the observed silence, as the audience stood with their heads bowed, Tom started coughing vigorously. Andy patted him on the back, gently rubbing it when he stopped coughing. As Tom mouthed a 'thank you' to Andy, he noticed a middle-aged woman staring directly at them with a scornful frown. She wore a black t-shirt with a large American flag wrapped around a bald eagle. As the silence ended, she walked up to them in a determined beeline.

"That was so damned disrespectful! I hope you're both ashamed of yourselves."

Tom looked shocked. "Excuse me, but I was coughing. There's nothing I can do about that!"

"You know what I mean! I saw the way he touched your back and how you two queers looked at each other! This isn't some fag rally - this is a patriotic memorial for the dead!"

In the same indignant tone he used towards the two homophobes the night before, Andy said, "We've come out here for the same goddamn reason you did and like you, we have every right to be out here. We're loyal citizens just like you! Being gay doesn't change that one bit!"

The woman looked disgusted by his words and stormed off, nudging people out of her way. Andy's tone and the mention of the word 'gay' silently resonated amongst those in earshot and as the speech finished, Andy and Tom left the crowd and took a short walk across the river to the park they passed the night before. They sat down on a wooden bench and Tom put his arm around Andy, pulling him close. Andy was still visibly flustered by the confrontation.

"Don't let her get to you."

"I'm sorry, but it really pisses me off when people aggressively throw the word 'patriotic' around. These days the only time people use it is to bully someone into a defensive position they have to crawl out of. It's people like her that make the rest of the world both laugh at American nationalism and fear the fact that we all so publicly accept it. ... You know, just before the moment of silence, when the speaker talked about 'remembering the fallen' and 'honoring their memories', I started thinking about my mother. I thought about how she used to hold our family together and it really made me miss her. I tried to mentally picture what she looked like when she smiled, but all I could recall were vague features and a blur of the color of her hair. But though I couldn't picture her face, I could remember exactly what her laugh sounded like and the memory of it nearly made me cry. Then as you started coughing, I instinctively put my hand on your back and then my mind was flooded with the thought of how happy I was to have you right there with me. I'm sorry for getting so crazy back there. I don't know why but I'm just really sensitive right now."

"It's probably all the change you're having to get used to."

Andy just shrugged his shoulders and squeezed Tom's hand, holding it as the crowd dispersed and walked past towards their cars.

15

Roberto hung asleep over his father's shoulder as they walked in the front door in the late afternoon. Susan heard the door slam and she leapt out of bed to greet them.

"Sorry we're so late honey. We were on the paddle-boats for a while and then I bumped into a couple guys from the department."

Roberto looked a bit sunburnt while Susan's father seemed very mellow. As Susan leaned in to gently kiss Roberto on the cheek, she could immediately smell beer on her father.

"Daddy, I'll take Robby to his bed so he can have a little nap before we do dinner."

"Okay sweetie. Don't forget we're joining the neighbors later for a barbecue out front."

"I know, Dad."

Susan carried Roberto to his room and sat him down on his bed to take off his shoes, but he stopped her to do it on his own. As Susan tucked him in, she asked, "Did Daddy have a lot to drink?"

"Only two. They said he was driving. I'm tired, Susie."

José had a few more beers before he and his family joined the barbecue. That evening, they spent most of their time getting to know a young family who recently moved in. Tim had just spent the last few years in the Army and was now studying to be a paralegal at the local university and his wife Lee was a hospice nurse who worked with the elderly. As Tim and José shared a few beers, Susan and Lee snuck away for a chat.

"So Susan, now that you're finished with high school, what are your plans?"

"I really don't have any plans right now."

"What about college or work?"

"Well, I thought about college but right now my priorities are here with my family. I'll probably get a job soon to help out with the bills. Dad doesn't work right now but we still have some money saved up."

"What does your dad want you to do?"

"I don't know. We don't really talk about it."

"You should. You seem like a clever girl. It would be a shame for your smarts to go to waste."

Minutes later, Susan saw Tom's car pull into the far end of the parking lot and she ran over to greet him. Only when she got to the car did Susan realize Tom had a passenger with him. "Hi Mr. Woodbine!"

"Hi Susan. How are you?"

"Great thanks!" She turned to Andy and asked, "Who's this?"

"This is Andy."

Susan looked at Tom coyly. "Is he your boyfriend?"

Tom squirmed speechlessly.

After a few seconds Andy said, "Yes. Yes I am."

"I'm Susan." Susan thrust her hand out to Andy. "It's a pleasure to meet you Andy."

Andy took her hand. "And you Susan."

Tom looked over at the barbecue and saw the faces of his neighbors all turned towards him. "Right. Well I've got to get inside and make us something to eat. It was good to see you Susan."

"And you too Mr. Woodbine."

"Susan, you're not my student anymore. You're an adult. Please call me Tom."

"Okay, Tom."

Tom and Andy gathered a couple bags of groceries from the back seat and headed inside. As Susan walked back to the barbecue, she noticed a few of her neighbors were staring at her strangely. They continued to do so until the barbecue ended a couple hours later as the sun set. With their bellies full, the Ortegas dragged themselves back to their apartment to collapse. Roberto went straight back to bed, still exhausted from his day out. Susan lied down on the sofa next to her father with her head resting on his lap. The thin, milky glow of the waxing crescent moon that filled the room was instantly overwhelmed as the television was switched on.

"Daddy, when do you think you'll go back to work?"

"I don't know sweetie. Soon I hope." He was still tipsy but this unsolicited question obviously touched a nerve.

"I think I want to go to college." José sunk into the sofa. "I don't know exactly what I want to study yet but I'd like to at least give it a try."

With his head in his hands he said, "Honey, you know we don't have the money to send you."

"We would if I went to a cheaper local college and you went back

to work. I could even get a part-time job to help out. We could then stop living off the life insurance money and we'd still have more than enough. I've done all the math for it!"

"I'm sorry, but it's just not going to happen right now."

Susan sat upright and shouted, "God, you're so selfish!"

"Excuse me?!"

"You just want me to stay here and take care of you and Robby from here on out so you can drink all day and feel sorry for yourself, don't you!"

"Susan, stop this now or else I'll -"

"You'll what? Hit me? Go ahead, hit me! At least then I could stop feeling sorry for you." José was speechless. "I'm just so sick of this! I don't mind looking after Robby, but I'm done pampering you. If you care about me, you'd at least try to see things from my point of view."

"You think I don't?! I feel horrible for having to rely on you all the time."

"Then do something about it!" Susan stormed out of the living room straight to her bedroom, slamming the door and locking it behind her. She sat down on her bed, breathing heavily, and tried to compose her thoughts, but after a few minutes she turned off the lights and sat in the middle of her room in the dark. She shut her eyes and began to pray silently.

Dear Lord, why do I feel so alone? I'm doing everything I can to be a good person, but am I doing your will? Please, God, just give me some sort of sign. Just this once, could you speak to me? It's not like I'm not asking you for money or fame or anything like that - I just want some clarity. I just don't see how you can be so clear to everyone else and not me! Please just give me something!

Susan kept her eyes closed and thought about Pastor Simmons. He had been the pastor of their church as far back as Susan could remember and he was always willing to listen to her when she had a question. Even though she knew and understood his reasons for retiring, she suddenly began to feel as if she was losing one of the only people she could turn to for guidance.

As Susan finally opened her eyes and allowed them to adjust to the dark, she saw familiar lights dancing across her bedroom walls. In a daze, she ran to the window. Susan wrenched the mini-blinds open and watched as Tom ran out of his house to the landing, guiding the paramedics up the stairs. The look of helpless horror on Tom's face sent Susan sprinting out of her room.

16

In the hot afternoon sun, Tom and Andy walked from the town park to the university grounds. Across from the unpopulated gardens was a large, brown brick chapel surrounded by the campus administrative buildings. On the display board outside the chapel was a listing of the different service times and a small plaque inscribed with gold letters that briefly outlined the school's incorporation of the 'Baptist Ministry' into the curriculum.

"So is chapel attendance mandatory for students here?" Andy asked.

"It *is* a Baptist university."

Andy scoffed.

"So - here's a nice light question we've managed to avoid so far," Tom said, smiling like a mischievous child. "Where do you stand on religion?"

Andy looked as if the question had punched him in the stomach. "Uh, well, I think I mentioned the other day that I was raised Catholic, but I got fed up with it years ago. Just after I finished law school I did the typical backpacking trip through Europe which ended in Rome. I was still a devout Catholic then and felt a duty to visit the Vatican while I was there, so I jumped in with one of the countless guided tour groups. We were taken around the grounds to all of the usual photo-op tourist spots, but for me, the sights were so otherworldly that even with a camera around my neck I didn't have the mental wherewithal to take a single picture. When we entered St. Peter's Basilica, we were taken to a massive painting, or at least we all thought it was a painting, that was as tall as this chapel here. The tour guide had

117

this wry smirk on his face as he said, 'Closer, closer,' and shuffled backwards to this painting, and one by one, everyone in our group gasped as we realized it was actually a mosaic full of blue and gilded tiles. I found it strange that as our guide casually presented all the 'priceless' treasures of the Vatican, he seemed to have an extensive knowledge about their worth. Now don't get me wrong, the Vatican was stunning - but it was obscene. It's like they had collectively disregarded the Christ that threw the money-changers out of the temple and profanely replaced him with a gold-plated, jewel-encrusted likeness. It was all I could think about on the flight home. I went into the airport chapel on my first lay over and sat down alone just to be away from all the extra noise and distractions. I found myself surrounded by the familiar ceremonial images and icons I knew all my life - and for the first time, I felt nothing for any of it. Since then, I've been calloused towards the organized side of religion in general, but I think I still *feel* something for the spiritual side of things. I'm not sure what that feeling is or where it's directed, but I still have some lingering regard for, well, *something*. ... I don't know, it's hard to put into words."

"There is a word for that feeling," Tom said. "It's called the *numinosum*."

"Beg your pardon?"

"Gosh, I'm going to sound like such a geek -"

"Ha! I think we're past that."

"- but back in college, I read a Jung essay about the different forces that weighed upon the *Self*. Jung used several forms of the word 'numinous' to describe the intangible feelings we have that overwhelm us, usually regarding spiritual things. He said it was an 'experience of the subject independent of his will' and was typically linked to the feelings of synchronicity. He argued that organized religion actually kept people from experiencing these numinous feelings because the churches regimented an

118

individual's involvement in their own spirituality. What annoyed me was that the entire essay was a huge cluster of words that essentially said the numinous wasn't able to be described by words. I remember feeling even more confused about a sensation I myself had never felt."

"That's interesting," Andy said, "though I'm not sure that feeling I'm talking about is necessarily spiritual. I don't mean to further confuse you - but I definitely think there's something linking synchronicity with that sense of *something*. I don't like telling people about this because they always treat me differently afterwards. You're going to think I'm crazy but -"

"I think we're past that." Tom smirked and put his hand over his own mouth.

"- but all my life I've had these strangely detailed dreams that would unfold in reality exactly as they did when I was asleep."

"Okay..." Tom's eyes narrowed in doubt, but he gestured for Andy to continue.

"I can always tell the difference between a premonitory dream and an ordinary one. First, a strong sense of calm overtakes me in the dream and I begin to feel weightless. Then, everything falls silent except for the conversation at hand. If there are people in the dream, I'm somehow alerted to which ones are important, and all my attention is automatically focused onto them. Even though I'm a part of the events that unfold, everything that happens in these dreams feels totally out of my control - including my own actions and thoughts. You may have noticed that I keep notebooks all over the house - mostly in places where I know I may fall asleep or daydream. The first details I usually remember when I wake up are colors, and I write them down straight away. I'll sometimes remember a few key phrases or topics of conversation and they're next on the page. Very rarely I'll recognize one of the people in the dreams and what they were wearing, but I can never quite remember where the dream itself takes place. Since I'm quite dazed and uncoordinated when I wake up, the handwriting in all my notebooks is atrocious. I'll sometimes go through the notebooks a day or two later and have no idea what any of my words say. The funny thing about all these weird dreams is that they're almost always about something totally insignificant like a conversation in a bank or a meal with someone, but the sensations are always very strong when I feel déjà vu and I can always recognize when they start transpiring in reality. I immediately get that powerful sense of calm and then I start remembering all of the details from before. Usually I'll remember something incidental like the timing of a phone call and who's calling or I'll announce a stranger entering the room and know what they'll be wearing.

"One time, I was in the car with my wife as I was driving to pick up her father to drive him to the airport. We were just a few miles from his house when my wife started rattling on about her laptop and the familiar feeling of weightlessness hit me in the chest. The shock of it nearly made me drive the car off the road. My mind was instantly flooded with the memory of a dream in which I had the exact same conversation with my wife. She was wearing the same jacket and dress from the dream and I knew what I'd find when we got to her father's house. As if I was possessed or something, I remember I interrupted her and said, 'Your father's had a stroke - I'm going to take him to the hospital.' She started screaming at me right away, rightly so, and called me all sorts of horrible things. But right when I got to the house, I saw her father laying face-down in the front yard. Without missing a beat, I got him in the car and drove him straight to the hospital. My wife sat in the back seat holding and caressing him; they were both totally silent for the entire ride. Occasionally, she looked up to glance at me in the rear-view mirror, and I can still remember the glassy expression on her face.

Her dad survived the stroke but he never fully regained his coordination."

"Fuck."

"So because I feel I've seen or experienced things in a dream before they actually happen, however inconsequential they may be, I don't really believe in the linear arrow of time. I'm well aware that my stance on this has been proven wrong by sheer logic and every law of science, and that the very existence of things like entropy or gravity reduces my argument to fantasy. But what this knowledge does is it leaves me feeling like I've somehow been cheated by my own mind and the experience itself - that is until the next time it happens and I'm totally overcome by something I know can't be logically true. Does this make any sense?"

Tom paused to take it all in. "Obviously I can't personally understand all that you've experienced, but I think I get what you're trying to say."

"Good - because I barely do! What about you?" He poked Tom's chest. "Where do you stand on all this *numinous* mumbo-jumbo?"

Tom said, "Well, I didn't have a very religious upbringing. We went to church regularly but Mom and Dad never really talked about the teachings at home - unless we got in trouble. I really don't think about religion, God, the afterlife, or any of that stuff until someone else brings it up."

"Are you open to any of it?"

"I don't really believe in God, but I'm definitely not a dyed-in-the-wool atheist. In college I went through a phase of reading loads of militantly atheist books and, while I found them compelling and rather funny, I got the sense that they were mostly just reactionary to the faith-based stuff."

"What about fate?"

"It's just a word to me."

"I somewhat believe in fate, but not in some sort of set predestination that's totally beyond our control. We're constantly presented with opportunities and choices throughout our lives, and we're the ones who ultimately decide whether or not to take them, but I think fate presents us with those few really big, pivotal choices that can totally change our paths."

"I don't know," Tom said. "I guess I just need to experience something to put any credence towards it. What's real to me is the fact that I've seen films and heard songs that have moved me more than anything I've ever experienced at church or read in a spiritual text - and I'm fine with that. I don't need a promise of an afterlife to get through this existence and make the best of it. I'd like to think that I would be open to a belief in the supernatural or whatever you want to call it, but so far nothing has really touched me."

At this, Andy grabbed Tom's behind and asked, "Do you feel touched now?"

Tom rolled his eyes and said, "Praise the Lord Almighty - now I'm a believer."

"Something tells me that the local fold wouldn't necessarily approve of this kind of conversion."

"I think you may be right, Brother Andy."

Tom held Andy's hand and they walked on through the deserted campus. The late afternoon sky reddened and the sweet, smoky smell of Texas holiday barbecues filled the air. They walked back to Andy's house for water and a spare set of clothes for Andy before setting off to Tom's apartment for the night. On the way there, they stopped at the supermarket for salmon, vegetables, and a couple bottles of white wine. As they drove through the gate at Tom's apartment complex, Andy was entranced by the sight of flames bursting upwards from the communal grill pit.

"Looks like your neighbors are having a gathering! Should we join them?"

Tom cringed and said, "I don't particularly get along with my neighbors. One guy's super homophobic and gives me a really bad vibe."

"You know what they say about the homophobes - they all seem to have gay issues of their own. He probably just wants to sleep with you."

"Oh god, that's such a horrible visual."

After a brief chat with Susan, they walked up to Tom's apartment. Tom laughed as he closed the front door, realizing that now everyone must know he's gay.

Andy asked, "What's so funny?"

"I was just thinking about the neighbors. I'm sure they're gossiping away about us right now."

"Is that such a bad thing?"

"No, not really. I just like the thought that the is-he-or-isn't-he debate should be over for good." Tom set the grocery bags down on the countertop. "So, would you like me to give you the tour?"

"Nothing would make me happier."

It took them less than a minute to walk through Tom's tiny apartment. Andy laughed and shouted, "Oh wow!"

"What, the waving cat thing?"

"No, the picture! You look just like your father!"

If Tom's hair was black and he put on a little weight, he and his father would be identical.

"How old were you when this was taken?" Andy asked.

"We took it just before I got my degree, so I must have been twenty-one. We didn't really have many family photos, so one day Mom was insistent on booking a professional session. It was such an awkward afternoon. I remember her nearly fainting when they handed us the bill at the end, but I think the bright lights and inhaling loads of hair spray played a big part."

Andy poured them each a glass of wine then walked to the stereo. "What should I put on?"

"Anything you like."

As Tom began chopping vegetables in the kitchen, Andy shuffled through his several shelves of books and CDs. He slipped King Creosote & Jon Hopkins' *Diamond Mine* in the stereo, filling the tiny apartment with the soft chatter of a Scottish café. The bubbly hum of people chatting over a piano placed gently in the mix fused perfectly with the searing sounds of stir-fry in the kitchen. The café's hubbub slowly faded out and the wash of the sea filled the room through the speakers as Andy leaned back into the sofa and closed his eyes in sheer peacefulness, soothed by the singer's gentle Scottish brogue. The short album looped once more as they ate the meal at Tom's compact breakfast table. Afterwards, with full bellies and wine at the ready, they moved onto the sofa and laid next to other silently until the music stopped.

"I really love your little apartment, Tom."

Tom rested his head on Andy's chest and squeezed him. "That's the wine talking. It's a shit-hole."

"I'm serious. I can't think of anywhere else I'd rather be."

With another bottle of wine, they laid on the sofa and watched the daily highlights from the first round at the French Open. A commercial break began with a CGI explosion advertising the latest Hollywood mega-hit.

Tom said, "A friend and I meet up pretty regularly for nights out at the cinema, and when it comes to choosing what to see, we have one rule: We never watch a film that has cars flying over other cars in the trailer. Having said that, the last blockbuster we saw seemed to have nothing *but* cars flying over other cars, planes flying through buildings, or people jumping over lava. It was the disaster movie to end all disaster movies and we figured if we were ever going to break our rule - this was the film. We thought we'd bring a small bottle of scotch to dull our senses and make the viewing more enjoyable, but it just didn't work. After thirty minutes or so, we finished the bottle and walked out of the cinema."

Andy knocked back the last of his wine and asked, "Did the film mention anything about the Mayan calendar?"

"Briefly. Why?"

"Well, I was really caught up in the whole 2012 thing and the public obsession around it."

"You didn't actually believe any of it, did you?" Tom asked as he muted the television.

"Well, there was nothing there to believe or disbelieve - I was just intrigued by the conspiracies themselves and the reactions people had to them. Loads of people were so fascinated by the Mayan calendar ending on December 21, 2012 that they didn't really stop and research if it even meant anything."

"Did it?"

"It was just the end of the calendar's cycle - nothing more - but even though there was nothing concrete behind it, people gave the date power and relevance. Internet chatter turned to plots, plots to schools of thought, and then Hollywood predictably stepped in to take its cut before everyone else saw the opportunity to cash in. I even saw a deodorant advertised as '2012 - Final Edition'! The energy that was put behind it was incredible, and it even started to make me wonder if something could actually come from it. In the span of a couple months I became obsessed about the Mayan culture and even convinced my wife to go with me to Mexico to attend one of the massive end-of-the-world parties at a Mayan pyramid the day the calendar ended."

"Did the people there actually expect the world to end?"

"Only a few. The rest were there to party, but even then

everyone seemed like they were still somewhat entertaining the thought of impending doom. Nobody knew what time the calendar change actually came into effect so the vast majority was staying awake and going even loopier because of sleep-deprivation. If you travelled all this way, you'd never want to sleep through the end of the world."

"Guess not. Did you stay up?"

"I was probably the worst one there. The line between being fascinated by a theory and being won over by it had totally blurred in the heat of the situation and I didn't sleep for over three days. My wife was fed up with my endless loop of internet forum browsing, strong Mexican coffee, and pointless speculating so she justifiably left me at the hotel and headed back home. I stayed for another couple of days and watched from my room's balcony as people slowly left the village, and I started imagining about where these people came from and what lives they led, and how they could be convinced by the vague theories that brought us to Mexico. Ultimately I was trying to understand what had made me turn so neurotic. After an unplanned nine hour nap on the balcony, I woke with an awful sunburn and a theory. Bear with me on this: I believe when an idea or teaching gets stuck into the imagination and subconscious of any group of people, it becomes much more than just a concept and can develop and mutate quickly. Religions, political movements, even rock and roll are proof. We're now so connected with one another that the divide of distance means nothing to the expansion of an idea. Words, images, sounds, videos, and news events spread faster than we can keep up with and can spread to an ever-growing connected audience. Because we're quicker to learn about the world at large, the first things to make headlines are conflicts, outbreaks, economic crises, natural disasters - anything that affects human beings on a large scale. The news outlets are quick to report these because they know that we as an audience instinctively care about what's happening to our fellow man. And now, because we're so quick to learn about these events, it's easy to interpret that the world around us appears to be deteriorating at an alarming rate - even though we're in a statistically untroubled era when compared to times like the conquering of the Americas. And this leads to more end-of-days preachers making vague links to prophecy and then getting loads of publicity when they announce a date when the world will end. In this case, a specific date was given seemingly at a time when the tensions of the world couldn't be higher."

"Quick question: do you wear a tin foil hat to keep *The Man* from reading your thoughts?"

Tom winced as Andy pinched him in the side and said, "I know it all must sound silly to you, but when we lend credence to something abstract there really is no telling where it can lead. There's always the possibility that we ourselves will cause events just from the sheer expectation of it."

"I suppose..." Tom stood from the sofa and stretched as he yawned. "Anyway, I think you're adorable when you get worked up like this."

Tom ruffled Andy's hair before walking to the kitchen for another bottle of wine. As he closed the refrigerator door, Tom watched as Andy clumsily leapt from the sofa and sprinted to the bathroom. Tom set the wine down and ran after him, and just as he got to the open door of the bathroom, he saw Andy vomiting into the toilet. "Jesus Christ! Andy, are you alright?"

Andy held the rim of the toilet and stayed still for a moment. He took some tissue, wiped his mouth, and looked at Tom with tears in his bloodshot eyes. "I don't know. I was feeling fine and then out of nowhere I had the strongest urge to puke."

"God, I hope I haven't poisoned you!"

"No, my stomach didn't feel bad. I just felt really disoriented and then my body told me that I had to puke - so I ran." Andy held his head in his hands as he quivered on the bathroom floor. "I don't think I need to vomit again, but my head is fucking killing me. I think I need some of those headache pills."

Tom helped Andy up and put his arm around Andy's shoulder to walk him back over to the sofa. Tom heard the crack of the pills through the blister-pack as he quickly walked to the kitchen for a glass of water. He handed Andy the glass and sat next to him, feeling the light tremble of Andy's body through the cushions. As Andy brought the glass to his lips with his left hand, his right hand began to shake violently. Andy's face seemed wrought with terror before his features fell limp and his eyes rolled back in his head. He dropped to the floor in front of the sofa, glass in hand, and his body fiercely thrashed about. His knees slammed into the coffee table and his head started to bash into the bottom of the sofa. Tom intuitively fell to the floor and put his hands over the wooden sofa legs to protect Andy's head, but his lip was already split and blood soon spattered across Tom's hands and the carpet. All Tom could do was wait for Andy to stop - but the convulsions kept coming. Tom grabbed the pillows off the sofa and quickly placed them on all the rigid corners around Andy's shuddering body, grabbed his phone, and dialed 9-1-1.

"Hello? My boyfriend is having a seizure! I don't know what I should do. He's been seizing for a couple minutes and he's not stopping."

"Sir, where do you live?"

"I live in Belle Oaks apartments on East Avenue J, just behind the elementary school."

"An ambulance will be there shortly sir."

Andy kept convulsing for another thirty seconds or so before his body lied limp. The cut on his lip was beginning to swell and his bare legs were battered and already started to discolor. Tom fell to the floor and stroked Andy's dozing head until the ambulance arrived. Tears came to his eyes and Tom realized he had never felt so terrified.

17

A tiny shard of glass pierced the skin of Susan's right heel as she ran across the parking lot in her bare feet. She pulled it out mid-stride and threw it into the grass, then limped up the stairs to Tom's open door. As she entered the apartment, Susan saw Tom distraughtly giving details to a short male paramedic at the far end of the sofa. Susan ran up to Tom and threw her arms around him.

"What happened?"

Tom rubbed his eyes and said, "He just started shaking then fell to the floor!"

A strange nostalgia washed over Susan as she hugged Tom, squeezing his shaking ribs. All the memories of her night spent on his sofa - the smell of the tea, the melodies of the song, the feel of the sofa's springs in her back - they all came flooding back. Susan turned behind her and looked at Andy's bloodied shins as he lay on the floor, parallel to the sofa, while another paramedic knelt next to him and shone a small light into his eyes.

Susan gasped loudly she recognized the paramedic who brought her mother into the ER the night she died.

"It's you!"

The paramedic turned to face Susan and froze as her face immediately drained of color. After a few seconds of rattled staring, the paramedic seemed to come around and turned back to tend to her patient.

"We need to get him to the hospital. Gary, will you help me get him downstairs?"

Most of the neighbors watched from their doors as Andy was carefully carried down the narrow concrete stairs to the ambulance. Tom and Susan walked closely behind the paramedics, watching their every move. As they secured the gurney in the back of the ambulance, the female paramedic turned to Tom with a solemn look and said, "I'm really sorry but only family can ride in the ambulance to the hospital."

"But that's insane! I'm all he has!"

"Look, I don't agree with the rule but it's company policy and I'm not risking my job over it. Plus, I know that my driver won't leave with you in the vehicle. We're headed to the ER in Temple - do you know where that is?"

"I do, but I've had a little to drink. I don't think I should -"

"I'll drive," Susan interrupted.

The paramedic looked at Susan very seriously. "Fine, but drive carefully and don't speed. There's a family-only policy regarding visitors in the ER, but I'll talk to the nurses and try to make sure you can get through. I can't make any guarantees though."

"I understand. Thank you."

Susan ran back to her apartment for the car keys in her purse just as the ambulance drove away. As she crept in through the front door, she kept a watchful eye on her father, who was asleep on the sofa, oblivious to the crisis outside. Susan tiptoed past her room to Roberto's and saw him fast asleep as well. She slid a pair of shoes on, grabbed her purse, and quietly left the apartment.

Susan and Tom parked outside the ER and Tom sprinted ahead through the automatic glass doors. As Susan stepped out of the car, she quickly realized she had parked exactly where she knelt the night of her mother's death. A sense of urgency prompted her to run on ahead, but as she neared the doors she remembered watching her mother being wheeled into the hospital. The dancing ambulance lights in the covered parking bay and the glow of the moon lit the ER doors exactly as before and Susan suddenly felt powerless to the motion of the world around her.

As she walked in the door, Susan spotted Tom and the paramedic waiting for her at the ER's secured entrance.

The paramedic said to Tom, "They're not supposed to do this sort of thing but it's been an odd day here at the hospital. If anyone else asks who you are, you tell them that you're Andy's brother." She then put her hand on Susan's shoulder and said, "And you're his daughter. Understood?"

They both nodded.

"If you don't, you'll get yourselves, me, and the nurse who's letting you past in serious trouble."

The paramedic walked them to a small empty room and closed the door once they entered. The windowless room smelled of sour chemicals reminiscent of a photographer's dark room.

She said, "Right now, Andy's having a CT scan. They'll bring him back soon. You can either wait here or you'll have to go back into the waiting room and I can't guarantee that you'll be able to get back through. My partner's waiting for me outside."

As the paramedic started to leave the room, Susan grabbed her hand. "Wait! What's your name?"

"I'm Laura - and you're Susan. I haven't forgotten about you."

"Can I walk outside with you?"

Laura looked at Tom for approval, but Tom sat expressionlessly in shock next to the empty hospital bed. He looked pale and hadn't said a single word in the last half hour. Susan and Laura followed in reverse the same path they took months before, saying nothing to each other until reaching Laura's parked ambulance. Laura's partner was on his cell phone a few paces away from the ambulance parking bay, gesticulating wildly with his free hand as he spoke.

Laura looked uncomfortable as they walked up to the ambulance. In an almost expulsive manner, she asked, "Was there anything in particular you wanted to talk about, Susan?"

Susan's gaze was directed to the parking lot where she and Laura embraced months ago. She remembered Laura shedding her bloody jacket and the tears that strolled down her face.

"I wanted to thank you for coming to my mother's funeral. I didn't get to say it at the time but it means a lot to me that you came."

"You're welcome."

"I've thought about you a lot since then. Every time I go to church, I imagine you're standing in the far corner like you did at the funeral, but in my head you're wearing the same uniform you're wearing now. I've never told anyone this. ... Sorry for being so weird."

"It's not weird. It's not what I was expecting to hear, but it's definitely not weird.."

"I'm just really happy to see you again," Susan said. "I knew I would some day. It's a shame we had to meet again like this."

"It's part of the job."

"Do you like what you do?"

"I really do," Laura said proudly. "It's hard work and a lot of the time it's difficult to stay emotionally distant enough to actually get the job done. Before this, I used to work in an office, but one day I was struck with the idea that I had to make a change. Becoming a paramedic is the best thing I've ever done. Why do you ask?"

"Well, now that I've finished school, I don't know what to do with my life. All I've been doing and all I can see myself doing right now is taking care of my family. My dad hasn't worked since Mom died, and I... I -" Susan's eyes filled with tears and she began to sob.

"There, there - it's okay." Laura said as she threw her arms around Susan, rubbing her back. Susan's tears rolled down Laura's reflective yellow jacket.

A call came in on the ambulance radio beckoning Laura and her partner away to a traffic collision.

"Oh jeez, I'm sorry but I really have to go." Laura scribbled down her phone number, gave it to Susan, and said. "Call me if you need someone to talk to."

The ambulance drove away and Susan walked back inside through the ER entrance. The same nurse that let her through earlier was on duty and didn't bat an eye as Susan entered. Everything looked just as she remembered from the night her mother died. Wiping her eyes, Susan walked down a hallway to where she found her father surrounded by the on-call doctors. She walked past the room where Tom waited for Andy reached a pair of white metal doors with reinforced glass windows at the end of the corridor. She peered through the small windows and saw a queue of about a dozen people filing towards the Intensive Care Unit. Towards the middle of the line was Veronica Taylor, a girl Susan recognized from school. Veronica was a small, plump girl with short blonde hair and an infectious giggle. Even though Veronica was two grades below, Susan knew her older brother Jason from four consecutive years of art class. Veronica helped as a model for one of Susan's final art projects of this past school year.

Susan saw tears streaming down Veronica's pallid face as she walked with the rest of what must have been her family. Susan pressed a large square button that opened the doors where she stood and called out to Veronica. Veronica turned her head to face Susan and jumped out of the procession, running to Susan with her arms stretched out.

"What's wrong Veronica?"

Veronica gasped as she spoke. "My brother. Jason. They're going to take him off life support. We're going to be with him."

"Oh my God! What happened to him?"

"Jason crashed his car and broke his neck Saturday night after graduation. He was awake yesterday but a... a blood clot must have travelled up to his brain. He had a stroke last night and there's been no brain activity for the last few hours. We wanted to wait until the rest of our family could get here before -"

Veronica cried and held on to Susan's shoulders as her knees buckled, bringing them both to the ground. Knowing that Jason was going to die was one thing, but seeing Veronica so distraught stirred something unfamiliar in Susan. The night nurses on duty watched as Susan helped Veronica to her feet, putting to good use all the practice she had helping her drunk father around the apartment. The nurses held the door and guided Susan and Veronica to Jason's small but filled room.

Veronica's family waited inside the room, circled around Jason's bed. Susan stood with the family as they watched Jason's still body regularly pulse to the rhythm of the machines around him. A short nurse in light green scrubs entered the room and introduced herself as the hospital's patient liaison. She calmly told the family the order in which the life support machines would be terminated and the different procedures that followed. Because Jason was an organ donor, his body would be taken away shortly after he passed away for harvesting, but the family would be given time with him before and afterwards. The liaison was very respectful and succinct in her delivery, and she gave her condolences to the family as she left the room. A young male nurse, barely over twenty years old, waited by the door for the liaison to finish her consultation before he entered carrying a small foil tube and a plastic bag. He trembled as he carefully walked betwixt Jason's family to the heart rate monitor, and as he switched the alert system off, a whimper from Veronica rippled through the room triggering several more sobs. The nurse then shuffled past Susan and Veronica to the ventilator and switched it off. The accordion-like pump visible through a glass cylinder stopped pulsing and the slow, regular rise and fall of Jason's chest came to a halt. The nurse quietly tried to tell the family he needed to move past, but no words came from his mouth as it moved. He couldn't make eye contact with anyone in the room as he slid through them to Jason's bed. He removed the lid from the foil tube, opened Jason's mouth, and squeezed a small amount of the clear lubricant substance inside. Susan noticed that Jason's lips were chapped to the point of splitting. The nurse slowly pulled the clear breathing hose from Jason's throat and tried to no avail to close Jason's gaping mouth. His lower jaw kept dropping down and his loose tongue slid to the left side of his mouth. The nurse's lips quivered as he realized he had done all he could and he left the room as silently as he entered.

Jason was now fully disconnected from the orchestra of devices that sustained him and Susan couldn't look away from the monitors that still displayed Jason's vitals. Jason's mother fell to her knees while holding his hand, weeping and screaming, "My son! My beautiful son!" Seeing her open affection and hearing the hurt in her voice brought more than just tears to Susan's eyes as the heart rate monitor slowly dropped to zero. Susan held her hand to her mouth and choked on the guttural sobs that gushed from within.

The nurses waited in another room, remotely monitoring the machines, and they swooped in just after the silent flatline. As the liaison reverentially reminded the family they would have a few more minutes with Jason, another male nurse came in to check Jason's pupils. He lifted Jason's eyelids and shined a small LED flashlight into his pupil to no reaction. Susan could see that the whites of Jason's eyes were slightly yellow and spotted with grey blotches. Seeing all this became far too much for Susan and she ran out of the room, racing down a flight of stairs and along a quiet corridor before slipping into a dark, empty patient room. With her back to the door, she took a series of deep breaths to try to calm herself, but each congested sniffle, gasp, and gulp shook her weary body. Susan felt her way through the dark room and sat in a vinyl armchair at the foot of the empty bed, wiping and closing her eyes. She pulled her knees to her chest, leaned back, and, slowly, sleep came to her.

18

For Tom, the time from calling 9-1-1 to sitting in Andy's empty hospital room was almost entirely a blur. He sat with his fingers weaved nervously through his hair trying to remember any of the details. A nurse arrived shortly after 10PM wheeling Andy in through the door. Tom leapt from his seat and ran over to the gurney to see Andy still unconscious. His upper lip was swollen and black in the right corner.

"How is he?" Tom asked.

"He's stable and should be fine for the night. We've run some head CT scans and a specialist will go over the results in the morning."

"So is there something wrong with him?"

"It looks like something has shown up on the CT scan, but we can't say what it is for sure until it's been analyzed. There's a backlog of scans for the imaging department to process because of the spike in incoming patients we've had today. Every Memorial Day sees a rise in domestic and traffic incidents, but this year's been especially bad."

"So should I wait here with Andy?"

"Since he's stable we'll be moving him out of the emergency room into a shared room on the third floor. Visiting hours are long since over so you can either wait in the family waiting area for the night or go home. You'll be able to visit him tomorrow morning at eight."

"Thank you."

Tom stood and kissed Andy on the forehead then followed the nurse to the waiting room. Whether it was shock, fear, or just general despondency that drained him, Tom was exhausted and had no trouble falling asleep across a row of chairs in the waiting room.

Tuesday, May 30

Tom is dreaming as the sun begins to rise. From another person's perspective about a hundred yards away, he sees himself standing on a nondescript beach. Gulls fly past him with their mouths agape, yet they make no sounds. Waves strike the beach with a low muffled tone that seems to shake the ground far beneath the surface. The noonday sky is a silvery grey striped with dense, menacingly dark clouds that seem ready to hail razorblades. Though the sun is obscured by clouds, a bright full moon hangs in the sky next to it as clear as can be. As a cold gust of wind tears over the beach and blasts Tom with sand, he realizes that though he sees himself from someone else's viewpoint, he is able to vicariously sense and feel what happens to his own body. His body suddenly feels a compelling urge to run from whomever is looking in on him. He can comprehend that every muscle and joint in his body seems locked and unable to move quickly. The other perspective seems to perceive Tom's vulnerability and runs after him. It throws Tom to the ground and swipes at his face leaving deep claw marks. Tom can't defend himself and lies on his back covering his bloodied face. The creature slashes at his stomach and devours the soft, steaming viscera inside. With a sharp metallic taste in his mouth, Tom keeps trying to wake himself up from the dream but can't. He's forced to watch himself savaging and being savaged.

Tom stirred awake on the green low-pile carpeted floor of the waiting room. The bright morning light hit him at eye-level as he sat up in one of the chairs of which he rolled out the night before. As he stretched his aching back, he rubbed his eyes and saw a shrunken old man in a pressed burgundy suit sitting across the room. The light faintly shimmered off his glossy polyester sleeves. The elderly gentleman looked at Tom in his disheveled state with a kindness and understanding Tom couldn't comprehend.

"Son, did you stay the night here?"

The events from the night before came flooding back to Tom. "Yeah, I guess I did. What time is it?"

"It's about half past seven. Visiting hours will start soon." The gentleman braced himself on his armrests and slowly stood. He picked up a canvas bag full of clothes and walked over to Tom. "Son, you look like you could really use a cup of coffee. I was just about to head over to the cafeteria - would you like to join me?"

"Thanks, I would. I'm Tom, by the way."

The gentleman wobbled as he giggled and held his angular, bony hand out for Tom to shake. "Nice to meet you Tom. I'm Gerry."

Tom and Gerry leisurely walked the empty, eerily quiet hospital halls to the cafeteria, where inside the tables seemed nearly full of nurses and staff having breakfast. The soft, dozy hum of low-volume morning chatter barely extinguished a small radio at the cashier kiosk while the smell of pastries and microwaved scrambled eggs made Tom's stomach growl. Tom reached his hands in his pockets and realized that he must have left his wallet at home.

Shit. "Sorry Gerry, but I'm going to have to pass on the coffee. I left my wallet at home."

"Don't worry about it - this is my treat. Besides, if anything you'll be keeping me company until I can see my wife." He held out his canvas bag for Tom to take. "Now go ahead and find us a table before the nurses snatch them all up."

Tom thanked Gerry and found a small table next to an obese nurse reading a gossip magazine. Carrying a tray with the coffee and two cheese danishes on small plates that clinked all the way, Gerry walked painstakingly slowly towards the table from the other side of the cafeteria. Tom nervously stood crouched next to the table, ready to catch anything should it fall.

At exactly 7:50, the cafeteria emptied and the nurses headed off to start their shifts. The clamor of heavy feet scurrying up to the waste bins carrying cutlery and dishes sounded to Tom like an avant-garde percussion section. Aside from the two cashiers, Tom and Gerry were the only ones left in the suddenly vast room. They sipped their coffee quietly as if to savor the silence.

Gerry broke the stillness. "Who are you waiting to see?"

"My brother Andy. He had a nasty seizure last night so they kept him here after a scan, but we don't really know what we're dealing with." Tom wanted to change the subject quickly. "So why's your wife in here?"

"She had her gallbladder removed a few days ago and they'll be releasing her later this afternoon. We were in the supermarket, in the baking goods aisle I believe, and she just clutched her stomach and fell to her knees. I tried to whisk her away to the hospital, but that stubborn woman insisted we finished our shopping first. I swear - nothing can kill that woman!"

Gerry's hand gently quivered as he stirred another packet sugar into his coffee. "Son, I can see how troubled you are, but you shouldn't worry too much about your brother's seizures. If they're something the docs can treat, they'll treat it. There's no need to get worked up over something if there's nothing you yourself can do about it. Life's too short to be spent stressed out."

Minutes later, when the hospital's visiting hours started, Tom and Gerry both headed upstairs to the third floor, waving to each other as they parted at the nurses' station. The on-duty nurse told Tom that Andy was in room 309 and, though he had been awake for some time now, Tom should try not to overstimulate him. As Tom walked into the room, Andy was sitting upright and laughing as he chatted to a nurse.

"Tom!"

Tom ran in and hugged Andy tightly. As he pulled away and sat at the foot of the bed, Tom noticed a small suture on the side of Andy's lip which lightly puckered the thin skin. The nurse quietly slipped out of the room.

"How are you feeling?"

"Well my head hurts like hell and my legs are sore, but aside from that I feel fine. This morning a nurse told me what happened but I don't remember any of it."

"You scared the hell out of me! Susan drove me over because they wouldn't allow me in the ambulance."

Tom had totally forgotten about Susan. *That sweet, sweet girl.*

"What do you mean they didn't let you on the ambulance?"

"They only allow family to ride in the ambulance - and I'm not exactly family, am I?"

"What a load of horseshit! I bet if you were my girlfriend they wouldn't have batted an eye!"

Tom put his hand on Andy's knee. "It's ridiculous but it doesn't matter. Has the nurse told you anything about your scan?"

"She said a doctor would come by later today once they've gone over everything. ... Tom, none of this feels real to me. I mean, I remember eating dinner at your house and then waking up this morning. Nothing else."

"Do you remember vomiting?"

Andy shook his head.

Tom said, "You ran into the bathroom right after you ranted about your fascination with the 2012 furore."

"Oh God, I don't remember any of that!" Tom watched Andy hold his pained face in his hands. The cord for the heart rate sensor on Andy's finger dangled next to a blue plastic bracelet.

"Look Andy, I'm sure everything will be fine. A nurse told me not to excite you so let's just relax. There's nothing we can do until your results get back so we might as well try our best to enjoy some downtime. Okay?"

Andy nodded and sat back in his angled bed. Tom did his best to remain outwardly calm, but the very same fear and anxiety he experienced the previous night still coursed through his body. He turned on the small television set and they watched a breakfast news program. The television's sound was routed through a small speaker built into the wired remote control for Andy's adjustable bed. A portly weatherman on screen announced the start of the tropical storm season and showed a graphic of a multicolored spiral storm approaching the southeastern tip of Cuba. By the end of the week, Tropical Storm Albert was predicted to move along the length of Florida before dissipating over Georgia and South Carolina. Tom held Andy's hand as they tried to distract themselves from the tormenting uncertainties within.

At 9:58, as the morning news programs came to a close, a very short doctor entered Andy's room holding a comically large clipboard.

"Mr. Strauss?" the doctor asked.

"That's me - the bruised one."

"I'm Dr. Harris from radiology. I have the results of your scan here. Is this man -"

"He's my boyfriend," Andy brusquely said,

The doctor didn't rise to Andy's remark. "Right. Do you want him here for the results?"

"Yes. Go ahead."

The doctor handed Andy a stapled series of paper printouts. "Here are the images. If you turn to the second page, you'll see a cross-section CT scan of your brain. Now," he pointed to a small white spot on the scan, "this is a mass."

Andy exhaled loudly.

The doctor continued, "We don't know what kind of mass it is nor can we know without performing a biopsy."

"What does that entail?"

"First off, let me assure you that a biopsy is a very simple operation. Because of the mass being on your parietal lobe near the back, the neurosurgeons would drill a tiny hole right here." He reached and touched Andy just above the cowlick swirl at the top of his skull. "The surgeons would then take a small sample or two of the mass for analyzing. They may even decide to remove or partially remove it then and there. We'll take a further MRI scan later today to give us a clearer view of what we're dealing with. When we deal with a mass that causes such strong symptoms, we typically move as quickly as we can to prevent any further growth."

"What does this part of my brain do and how can the growth affect that?"

"Well, the parietal lobe is split into regions. One deals with perception and sensation while the other handles taking sensory input and integrating it into the rest of the brain's functions. Specific types of verbal and visual memory loss as well as issues with bodily coordination are always concerns when dealing with this area."

"What sort of odds do I have of this being cancerous?"

"Like I said before, there is no way of knowing exactly what this is until a biopsy is performed." The doctor flipped through a few pages on the heavy clipboard. "I see you are part of the Greater Houston Preferred Provider Group."

"My wife and I signed up early last year."

"Wife?"

Andy rolled his eyes in exasperation. "It's a long story."

The doctor continued, "Anyway, your insurance coverage through that specific PPO would make any treatment like this outside of their own network rather pricey. Your scans taken here will be significantly covered but you'd be better off having the biopsy or further surgery in one of the specific hospitals in Houston. Do you have any further questions?"

"Just one: How long until I can leave?"

"Since you're stable and don't need any monitoring we'll be releasing you today after the scans. I have you booked in at 2:30 for the MRI, which should take no longer than 45 minutes or so. Then it's just a little bit of paperwork and you'll be done here. If you would like, I can contact your PPO now to put a rush on getting you an appointment in Houston."

"I would really appreciate that."

"Just so you know, a head MRI is painless but it's definitely not a very pleasant event. We'll place your head in a box-like brace and you'll have to remain perfectly still for the entirety of the scan. The slightest movement will cause a mis-scan and then we'll have to start the whole process again which adds to the cost. I only mention this because it happens more often than we'd like. To help with the noise we'll give you a set of earplugs, but the MRI machine is still pretty loud. If you need it, we can sedate you."

"I think I'll be fine."

"Great. Well I'll be back this afternoon to take you through to the scan. Try to take it easy until then, okay?"

Dr. Harris shook Andy's hand, smiled, and left the room. Andy sat back in his bed and let out a long, labored sigh as scores of concerns, possibilities, and dreads plagued his mind. He didn't even bother trying to outwardly conceal his anxiety.

"Thanks for being here," Andy said turning to Tom

"Hey, don't worry about it."

Tom paused to look Andy in his slightly teary eyes. He

grinned and said, "So Houston then? You know, I *have* been thinking about where to go for my summer break holiday..."

Andy squeezed Tom's hand tightly. "Would you go with me?"

"Of course I will."

Andy's painfully gloomy expression quickly faded. He was back to his usual joyful, although bruised, self.

"Tom, I've seen how bad I look right now - but you seriously look like hell. Please don't take this the wrong way, but I think you could really use a shower and a shave." He motioned towards a mirror across the room.

Tom's salmon-pink eyes widened at the sight of his wildly tussled hair and the stubble that had become bristle.

"I think I need way more than just a shower and a shave. Plus I could really do with a decent meal."

"Well why don't you go home for a little while? I'll be fine here on my own for a while."

"I could come back for your scan."

"You'd be bored senseless."

"Nonsense. I've got a good book I need to finish. I'll call my sister and see if she can come pick me up."

Tom stepped out into the hallway to call Sam. She answered and immediately said she was busy, but said to call her fiancée as he had the day off work. Sam hurriedly hung up and Tom pulled up his future brother-in-law's details on his phone. As the call connected, the contact's display picture showed the other Tom's face and shirt smeared with cake. The picture was taken on Sam's birthday after a gag gift of adult undergarments backfired. She was not amused.

"Hey Tom! How are you?

"I'm okay, but I'm in a bit of a pickle right now."

"What's up?"

"Well, last night Andy had a really bad seizure at my place and he had to stay overnight at the hospital. I'm here at the hospital now but I don't have a way to get home. I wanted to see if you could possibly drop me by my house."

"Yeah no problem! Is Andy okay?"

"A growth has shown up on a CT scan, so later today they're going to take some more scans and then go ahead with a biopsy."

"Shit, that's horrible. Look I'll be over there in about half an hour - is that okay?"

"That would be amazing Tom. I know Sam keeps a spare key of mine. I'll need it as my keys and wallet are inside."

"Yeah I know where the key is. So, Andy was over at your place last night then, huh?"

"Yeah.... I think we've started officially seeing each other."

"That's fantastic man! You know I think Andy's a great guy and I think you two make a great couple. Do you think he'd mind if I came in and said hello?"

"He'd probably appreciate the company. We're in room 309."

"Great stuff man. Later!"

Tom walked back to Andy's room and sat down at the foot of his bed. Tom placed his hand on Andy's knee and gently massaged it. He said, "My sister's fiancée is coming to get me in about half an hour. You remember Tom from the other night?"

"Yeah - the gorgeous one right? Who could forget him?" Tom squeezed Andy's knee and he yelped in pain. Tom forgot how bruised Andy's legs were after the seizure. Andy laughed and slapped Tom across the chest before he could apologize.

The other Tom arrived nearly an hour later in old clothes covered in paint. His hands and face had a few scattered streaks of bright pink paint as he had spent the day redecorating Shelley's bedroom. His visit was brief and full of laughter and benign flirting, and on leaving, he left Andy an ultimatum:

"Now, you'd better be in good health by our wedding next month. That's an order! Got it?"

Andy saluted him and shouted, "Sir, yes sir!"

As Tom walked into his apartment, his eyes were immediately drawn to the floor where Andy had his seizure. The sofa was slid far out of position and there was a light smattering of dried blood where Andy's face hit the corner. Tom spent the next few minutes scrubbing his carpet before having a shower. He stood motionless under the running tap after going through his usual shower routines. The hot, steaming water seemed to serenely paralyze Tom starting from his feet and working its way upwards, but the trance of the shower was quickly broken by his hunger. He turned the faucet off and walked to the mirror where he briefly stared at his foggy silhouette. As he dried his hair, Tom heard four soft knocks at the front door.

19

With a sharp inward breath, Susan woke up at the crashing sound of a medical trolley after being tipped over in the hallway. As syringes and other ephemera scattered down the corridor outside, Susan suddenly realized she was still in the hospital. She pulled her phone from her purse to check the time - 6:23 AM - and tried to recall exactly where she was in the building. Susan waited for a few minutes after the shuffling in the hallway died down before peeking her head out of the darkened room. Judging by the colorful decor, she guessed she was in the pediatric ward. Without any hesitation, Susan walked out of the room and followed a series of 'way out' signs, quickly reaching the parking lot then driving straight home. As Susan walked through the front door of her family's apartment, she saw her father asleep on the sofa with the comforter from Roberto's bed. She shut the door silently and walked down the hallway to her room. Roberto laid fast asleep in her bed, his shiny tussled mane spread across her pillow.

She thought, *Time for me to cut his hair again.*

Susan gathered a change of clothes from her dresser and walked to the bathroom for a quick shower. Afterwards, she walked back to her room with her damp hair in a towel to find Roberto sat on the side of the bed.

"I looked for you," Roberto said. "Where were you?"

"I had to take our neighbor Mr. Woodbine to the hospital."

"Is he okay?"

"He's fine. He needed to go see his friend who is sick."

"Sorry I slept in your bed."

"It's fine Robby. You don't have to be sorry."

"I gave my blanket to Daddy. He looked cold. Can we have breakfast?"

The sounds of Susan pouring cereal into Roberto's colorful bowl stirred their father awake. He yawned and stretched around the bend in their corner-unit sofa as the tiny comforter slid onto the ground. As José sat upright and rubbed his eyes, Roberto jumped onto the sofa next to him and hugged him.

"Susie went to the hospital."

"Susan... What's he talking about?"

Susan carried over their bowls and placed them on the coffee table. "I drove Mr. Woodbine to the hospital. His friend had a real bad seizure and the paramedics wouldn't let Mr. Woodbine ride in the ambulance."

"When did this happen?"

"Just after I went to bed last night. I saw the ambulance lights outside his apartment so I went to see what happened. You were already asleep and I didn't want to wake you up."

"Is everything okay?"

"I really don't know." Susan thought about her encounter with Veronica and quickly decided not to mention anything about Jason's death. "I wasn't allowed to stick around."

Mr. Ortega stood and walked towards the kitchen for a glass of water. "That's probably for the best. Susie, next time ask me if you want to leave the house that late, okay?"

Susan nodded and ate her cereal. She didn't realize how hungry she was until her stomach growled loudly as she ate the first spoonful. The family ate as they usually did: in front of the television, food in laps, cartoon characters flailing about on screen. With a slow exhale, Susan stopped mid-bite and appreciated the normalcy she normally deplored.

After a short refreshing snooze, Susan spent the next couple hours in her room researching different local nursing courses on her laptop. Something about the camaraderie of the nursing teams from the night before had sparked Susan's curiosity. As she read the course description for a Licensed Vocational Nursing program in Killeen, a car drove past her window and dropped Tom off at his apartment. Susan closed her laptop and walked out of her bedroom. From the sofa, Susan's father watched as she headed to the door.

"Where are you going?" he asked.

"Mr. Woodbine is back and I wanted to see how his friend is doing."

Her father closed his eyes and took a labored breath. "Listen Susan - I don't want you spending too much time with him."

"How come?"

"Well, you know what he is."

Of course I know what he is. "What are you trying to say Dad?"

"I just don't want you hanging out with a homosexual. That sort of thing isn't a good influence on you."

"That's ridiculous Dad!"

"Do you know what the Bible says about 'men who lie with men'?"

"Yeah - and I know what it says about drunks too!"

José scowled Susan and shouted, "Go to your room!"

"Dad I - "

"Go to your fucking room Susan!"

Susan stormed back towards the hallway and into her room. She slammed the door behind her and sat on her bed with her arms crossed. Roberto walked out of his room and softly knocked on her door but their father roared, "Leave her alone Robby! She's in trouble." Through the walls, Susan heard Roberto's little footsteps as he walked back to his room.

Twenty minutes or so passed before Susan heard her father

walk into the bathroom. Impulsively, she grabbed her purse, slid on a pair of sandals, and quietly walked out of her room. She silently closed her bedroom door and walked flat-footed to keep the sandals from slapping back at her heels. As Susan opened the front door, she heard the toilet flush and she quickly flung herself outside and walked the long way around the back of their apartment building to avoid passing her living room window. She knocked four times on Tom's door and heard him shout, "I'll be just a minute!" as his heavy footsteps shook the thin floor of his apartment and reverberated through to the suspended concrete walkway on which she stood. Moments later, Tom arrived at the door in a white robe with his wet hair slicked back.

"Hi Susan."

"Can I come in?"

"Uh, yeah I guess."

Susan quickly entered the apartment and sat down on Tom's sofa.

"I just need to get dressed," Tom said. "I'll only be a little while."

Susan listened as Tom rushed to get dressed. Minutes later, he walked back to the living room while vigorously towel-drying his hair.

"Is everything okay Susan?"

"Yeah fine. I just wanted to see how Andy was doing."

"Well, he's awake now, which is good. The doctors found a growth on his brain though. They're doing more scans in a few hours to see it better."

"Oh my god! I hope it's nothing major."

"Well, he's going to have a surgery done soon so they can analyze exactly what the growth is. We'll be leaving for Houston in the morning to consult with his doctors there." Tom saw the pained look of concern on Susan's face and kept talking. "What about you? Did you get home okay?"

"I stayed the night in an empty room at the hospital and got home early this morning."

"Your dad wasn't upset?"

"He had no idea I was even gone. He's been drinking more and more lately just passes out on the sofa every night. I don't think he even goes to his bedroom anymore unless he needs a change of clothes."

"Why'd you stay the night?"

"After I left the ER, I saw a friend of mine from school. Her brother was taken off life-support last night and I stuck around. I went into the ICU with her family and was there for the whole thing. I don't know why, but I just couldn't leave."

"Are you okay?" Tom asked.

"I think so. It's all a bit of a blur now." Susan seemed to look through Tom as if he wasn't in the room. After years of teaching, Tom was all too familiar with this blank expression.

"Hey look," Tom said, "I was about to make some lunch. Are you hungry?"

Susan nodded. "A little."

Using the last of the contents of his fridge, Tom quickly made several grilled cheese sandwiches and they ate quietly at his tiny dining table by the window. Susan stared outside as she ate, painfully squinting as the blinding reflections off the car roofs in the parking lot filled the room with their sharp white glare. Her mind flooded with the memory of the flashbulbs of her dream, yet something impalpably drove her to keep staring out at the light.

20

Tom sensed an uneasiness growing in the room. He knew the trauma of watching someone die must have been devastating, but Susan's demeanor had changed very suddenly over the last few moments. She started making less and less eye contact and seemed very reticent even in her glances. She even began to eat her sandwich slowly as if to delay any conversation.

"Is something bothering you, Susan?"

Susan looked up at Tom then down again to her plate. "I'm fine."

Tom thought, *She's not fine. She looks like she's ready to cry.* "Susan, I know you've been through a lot and I want you to consider me a friend whom you can tell anything. It's not healthy to hold everything in until it bursts out."

Without looking up from the plate, Susan smiled nervously and brushed her hair from her eyes. She breathed in deeply and sat back in the chair with her arms crossed. "I can't help it, and I know it's totally stupid, but last night I felt kinda responsible for Andy's seizure."

"What? Why?!"

"Well, I had a really rough day yesterday and a nasty fight with my dad, and last night I prayed and asked for some sort of message or sign. When I opened my eyes the ambulance was outside your apartment."

"What kind of sign were you asking for?"

"I don't know - just anything. Lately I feel like I've been doing everything I can to do good by the church and by my family, but it doesn't seem good enough. I just wanted some sort of message saying that someone up there was watching and listening."

"You know you had nothing to do with Andy's seizure. The growth in his brain must have been there for a little while now."

"I know... It's just the weird timing of everything I guess."

"Plus, I don't think that a loving God would give you a sign at the expense of another person's health."

"I guess so."

"Anyway, enough of that."

Tom looked across the room into the kitchen. He noticed that the white box from his classroom was still on the countertop at the far end of the kitchen. Without saying a word, he stood and walked to retrieve it. Susan watched as Tom shuffled around inside the box until something made a metallic clinking sound. He pulled out the hearts-and-stars chain Susan made and held it up for her to see. She blushed and hid her face in her hands.

"Oh my God, I can't believe you kept that!"

"It's the only thing I kept from this year really. You're more than welcome to it."

"No it's okay. I don't want it."

"You sure?"

"Definitely." Susan didn't tell Tom she made it from the wire hangers left over from her mother's clothes.

"Well I'll gladly hold onto it. It was easily the most creative project turned in on the Romeo and Juliet module. The blurb you wrote explaining how you turned the idea of 'star-crossed lovers' into a physical piece of art read like something at a gallery. I don't think I told you how brilliant I thought it was."

"Thanks I guess." Susan smiled bashfully and laughed.

Tom ran his fingers along the chain to make a jingling sound until one of the sharp edges grazed his thumb. He jumped and winced as the chain fell to the thin laminate floor, sending harsh, thin echoes through Tom's sparse apartment.

Susan left shortly after they finished eating. As she walked back towards her apartment, Susan turned around to Tom, waved, and shouted, "Give Andy my best!" At seeing Tom's fatigued face twist into a smile, Susan brightened up and lightheartedly pranced off with a merriness that Tom couldn't quite understand. In so many ways Susan was still just a girl, but Tom saw a maturity and purpose in her voice and actions that suggested otherwise. Now that he was alone in his apartment, surrounded by familiarities, Tom sat down on his sofa and put his feet up. He reached for his tablet and checked his email, which was mostly junk mail his mother forwarded on to him. There were two notifications of private messages from the dating site but Tom deleted them right away. He briefly checked his social networking sites and tried reading the daily news headlines, but the gravity of Andy's situation quickly took over his mind. Tom stood and went to his bedroom to fetch a change of clothes for Andy then gathered a few days worth of clothes for himself.

Tom arrived to Andy's room just as Dr. Harris began explaining the process in which the hospital would stream Andy's images in real time to the department in Houston.

"It will be as if they're in the room with us," he said.

As per hospital procedure, Andy was escorted from his room to the imaging department in a wheelchair. On the way, Dr. Harris politely suggested that Andy might want to relieve himself before the long scan. They stopped in front of the restrooms and Andy locked the brakes on the wheelchair and slowly stood; his flappy gown unfolded and exposed his backside as he rose. After only a few steps, Andy's thick legs wobbled and he leaned against the wall to regain his coordination, then giggled and steadily made his way to the restroom. As Tom heard the muted flush of the toilet through the walls of the MRI room, a man in ordinary clothing walked in and shut the door. It was David.

"Hi Tom! I didn't expect to see you here!" David took a brief glance at the medical chart.

"Uh, yeah. I'm, uh, here with someone. ... My boyfriend."

David's eyebrows raised in total surprise. "Boyfriend?! I thought you were single!"

"Well I was until very recently. It's a long story."

"It must be. I was only at your house just a few days ago!" Without missing a beat David said, "Hi Mr. Strauss, I'm David Matthews. I was the scan technician who took your scans last night and I'll be assisting Dr. Harris with your MRI. I've got to say - you look a hell of a lot better today. That lip was pretty bashed up when we scanned you last night."

"Thanks, I guess."

David smirked. "Now I don't want to rush you but your specialists in Houston are all set for the live linkup and will be assessing the images as we take them. Also, we've booked your consultation appointment in Houston for this time tomorrow afternoon. Is there anything we can do to make you more relaxed for the scan?"

"To be honest, I have no idea. Let's just crack on with it."

"Good man." David helped Andy onto the sliding platform bed, then positioned a foam stabilizer on Andy's head and tightened several small clamps to secure it. "I know we said this will take forty-five minutes or so, but since we know exactly where the mass is, we could finish sooner as long as you stay perfectly still throughout. You think we can knock this out in one take?"

Andy smiled and said, "Definitely. Do your worst, doc."

Tom squeezed Andy's hand before David escorted him into the windowless observation room. On a large flatscreen monitor, without any audio, they could see Dr. Harris speak briefly to Andy then move to a small control panel where he held a thumbs-up to the camera. At this, David flipped a series of switches and typed a short message to the Houston team in a window labeled 'Greater Houston Preferred'. Tom could feel a low rumble through the floor and watched the machine slide Andy into its open maw.

"So how long have you been seeing Andy?" David asked.

Tom's gaze didn't leave the screen. "Well you came over on Thursday and I met up with him on Friday after work."

"You sure move fast." With a stern face, Tom turned towards David. David raised his hands, smiled nervously, and said, "It's a joke Tom! I mean no offense."

Tom pinched David's taut side and turned back to the screen, saying, "You know, when I met up with Andy on Friday I had no intentions to date him or sleep with him. He sent me a message online looking for someone to show him around the area as he just moved here. The weird thing is that I normally wouldn't have replied to that sort of message. But there was just something nice and harmless about it that made me think 'what the hell?'. Since then we've spent every day together."

"So you're actually seeing each other then? Like a proper relationship?"

"Yeah I guess so."

"You guess so? What is that supposed to mean?"

"Well I've never really been in a relationship that wasn't purely sexual... No offense."

"None taken. Do you love him?" David didn't hesitate one bit to ask.

"What do you mean?!"

David coolly leaned back in the chair with his arms crossed. "Well you've spent the last few days together, you're here in the hospital as his significant other, and I hear you'll be taking him to Houston for his consultation and biopsy. Do you love him?"

Tom looked as if he was staring through the screen, through the image of Andy's still body laying in the yawning mouth of the MRI machine. He wondered, *How the hell am I supposed to know if I actually love him?*

"Hey if you don't want to answer, that's fine," David said, intensely focused on the screen. "I was just asking as a friend. ... You do know I'm your friend, right?"

"Yeah I know, sorry. I guess I've just never asked myself that question about anyone really. Still, everything feels different with Andy. It all feels really natural, yet so totally unfamiliar."

David watched his monitors for a moment then quickly responded to a short message that popped up on the screen.

"And all this stuff!" Tom pointed to the different apparatuses in the room. "These machines, doctors, diagnoses... It's all freaking me out a bit."

David rested his hand on Tom's knee. "I'm here if you need someone to talk to. It's not like we can't be pals just because we've had a bit of a past. It's like a close friend once told me: 'Sometimes you can only know who your friends are after you get the fucking out of the way.'"

"Is this from a friend you've slept with?"

Tom looked over at David, who tried his best to fight back a coy grin. They both laughed and turned back towards the screen to watch a seemingly endless flow of images materialize on the screen.

The scan had completed twenty minutes later and Tom watched as the MRI machine slowly expelled Andy's prone body. David answered a phone call and spoke in hushed tones about the initial impressions of these new scans and further steps to be taken. Tom's focus was still on the screen as the stabilizer was taken off Andy's head. Tom watched the discomfort on Andy's bruised face as he sat up and massaged his aching neck while Dr. Harris noiselessly chatted away. As the phone call ended, David stood and walked to the other room. With his eyes fixed on the screen in a near trance, Tom slowly followed David through the insulated door.

Do I love him?

21

"And sign here and here. Here. It's- It's May 29th. Yeah. No, just initial there. And at the bottom of the next page... Yeah. Okay. ... Okay, that's everything."

In a brightly-lit blue cubicle, Andy signed form after liability-free form with an admin assistant before he was allowed to leave the building. As he slid the tower of paper back to her, Andy stood up, stamped his right foot to the floor, saluted the woman, and spun to face the door. Tom hid his face as Andy marched out the front door.

"Shouldn't you be taking it easy?"

"That's what they say." Andy's stride grew quicker and more exaggerated. "I'm just really happy to be outside. There's nothing worse than spending hours upon hours in a hospital bed - especially when you're not sure what's wrong. And then all that damn paperwork to top it off... You know, I'm sure there have been embargoes and war declarations signed with less bureaucratic protocol and documentation!"

"Dr. Harris seemed really positive about this being treatable."

"And that's why I'm trying not to get so worked up about everything. This time yesterday, I walked through the park with you and was blissfully oblivious to this potentially harmful growth. Right now, all I want to do is soak up the sun and spend some time with you before we head to Houston."

The moment they walked through Andy's front door, he pulled Tom close and wrapped his arms around Tom's waist. As he pulled away, the shadows that fell on Andy's face made the cut on his lip seem deeper and the bruise under his left eye much larger and blacker. Tom took Andy's hand and they walked to the sofa and laid silently together until Andy stirred and chuckled.

"They're going to open up my skull and look at my brain. Isn't that weird?"

Tom didn't reply.

"The thing that regulates all my thoughts, feelings, bodily functions. The thing that's supposed to stay locked away behind bone, tissue, and God knows what else... They're going to have a look at it and take part of it out."

"Well, what did you think they were going to do?"

"Sorry, I guess I'm just coming around to the reality of all this." Andy stood and began to pace the room. "I mean, I knew this was serious enough, but they could be taking out the entire mass if they think it looks feasible - and it's not like I don't have faith in them or their ability to do things well. I just can't shake this nagging thought of 'what if things don't go exactly as planned?' Sure they've got the images of what it should look like in there," Andy said, tapping his temple, "but there's always something you just can't account for. ... Growing up, I never really feared death or the act of dying. I was raised to believe in heaven and hell and the idea that my soul or whatever it is would always live on beyond death from some all-knowing yet sentimental viewpoint. But at my mother's funeral, when I looked at her still body, I started thinking about my own physical death and the inevitable moment where my brain functions would cease for good. The thought of my own thoughts coming to an end scared me more than anything else ever has. Any time I try to imagine a never-ending nothingness, my mind seems to hit a wall and my heart starts to race. And now, what worries me the most about this entire ordeal is the chance that, after the surgery, my brain might not function as it does right now. I could wake up and be a totally different person, and that makes me feel something much more confusing and intangible than the thought of dying. ... I'm sorry to be like this, but it's all I can think about."

Tom put his hands on Andy's shoulders and looked him in the eyes and said, "I can't begin to imagine what this must be like for you, but it's pointless to get worked up about something over which you have absolutely no control. All we can do is get down to Houston and remain optimistic. That's well within our power, don't you think?"

Andy nodded and laid back down on the sofa with Tom, trying to calm himself, but as he forced a weak smile, his heart raced on. Tom could sense Andy's anxiety and, to break the mood, Tom went online to book two nights stay at a hotel near the Houston medical center. They then spent the twilight hours of the evening reclining in the canvas chairs on the back porch with a delivery pizza and a bottle of red wine. Andy's small portable stereo softly played *Metals* by Feist as they watched occasional fireflies flash and flutter by. As the sun set, the resonant din of cicadas faded and the night breeze slowly became too cool for their summer clothes. They gathered their glasses and a half-empty bottle, the stereo and their sandals, and entered the house. The rest of the evening slowly passed on with little conversation; their minds adrift on everything but each other's company. As Tom grew sleepier he thought he could physically sense Andy's heavy uneasiness cover him like a lead blanket, shallowing his breaths and pinning his clasped hands down to his lap. Though seated only a few inches from Andy, Tom felt miles away. In the corner of his vision, Andy watched as Tom's drowsy eyelids drooped and hid his pink eyes as he slowly nodded off, sliding further into his seat. As he watched, Andy felt a deep sense of gratitude and guilt for the stress Tom willingly endured. Andy stood, walked to Tom's side of the sofa, and crouched in front of him to gently wake him by stroking his hair. Tom shuddered as he came to and smiled as he looked upon Andy's bruised but gentle grin.

Andy thought, *There's no better way to know you're loved than getting a smile like that from someone waking up.*

Tom and Andy held hands as they walked to the bathroom to brush their red-wine-grey teeth. The sheer exhaustion of the last twenty-four hours hit Tom like a heavy wave making each of his brushstrokes more labored than the last. Andy tried his best not to laugh as he watched Tom clumsily spit into the sink before clambering to the bedroom to undress in an abandoned daze. Tom's clothes slid off him into a pile on the side of the bed and, within seconds of pulling the covers to his chin, he fell asleep. As Andy's cool, bare body entered the bed, Tom stirred but his eyes stayed shut as his right hand slid under the blanket to find Andy's. Within seconds, Andy felt Tom's grasp loosen as his entire body slowly relaxed bit by bit. In the process, Andy was slightly startled as he felt Tom involuntarily twitch a few times. Andy's wife used to do the same as she fell asleep and Andy couldn't help but smile as he reveled in both the new and the nostalgic.

22

Tom is dreaming. He feels a strong sense of solitude as he walks around his apartment in the warm afternoon light, sliding his socks along the cold laminate floor with distinct sibilant hisses. Every noise he makes seems unreasonably loud and resonates throughout the apartment as if it were many times larger than it appeared. He tries to say something aloud, but he can't speak - or at least he can't hear himself speak - yet every other sound seems to echo on and on. His own silence begins to frighten him and he hurries around his apartment desperately trying to find someone, anyone to help him comprehend what's happening, but each disorienting room seems more painfully loud than the next. In the short time it takes Tom to trek through his apartment, he realizes he is drenched in sweat. He slips to the floor silently panting, overwhelmed with a physically jolting loneliness. His gut wrenches and he curls on the floor in silent agony, gasping for air as he retches over and over, and suddenly, just as he feels his body can take no more, gallons and gallons of water begin spewing from his mouth like a ruptured water main. His body painfully convulses and contorts as his apartment rapidly fills with water.

Tom awoke as breathless and sweaty as he was in the dream. He wiped his brow and quietly glided out of bed without waking Andy. A thin glint of soft light through the balsa blinds lit the floor just enough for Tom to find his way through the room. After a shower, he tried in vain to read at the dining room table for half an hour until Andy's alarm rang. Tom watched with jealousy as Andy woke at six-thirty with his usual enthusiasm and vigor. Afterwards, they loaded Tom's car and wasted no time in joining the drowsy commuters on the misty freeway.

With his head back in the headrest, Andy stared out the passenger window at the morning fog. "This reminds me of a 7-hour bus ride I took in the UK from Manchester to Glasgow. Not the traffic or the scenery - just the blue, blurred edges to everything. I thought it would be fun to take the long route and travel by bus, but it was a nightmare. In Carlisle, just before the English-Scottish border, these two insufferable girls got on the bus and blabbed on and on about absolutely nothing, and it drove me crazy. I remember putting my headphones on just as the motorway snaked through a massive hill pass, then frantically flipping through my CD case for something loud and epic to drown them out. The only suitable piece I could find was the second disc of a Schoenberg opera. It's funny - I never could find the first disc. Anyway, just as the ending climax began to burst, the bus turned around the final bend through the hill pass and the sun flooded in through the massive pane windows along the side. Seeing it and feeling the instant heat was like watching a nuclear bomb exploding between two mountains. It was one of those extreme sensory moments I don't think I'll ever forget."

Andy froze as he said this. Still facing the window, he shut his eyes and slowly exhaled through his nose. "Well, I hope I never forget it."

Predictably, traffic worsened the closer Tom and Andy drove to Austin. Andy was still noticeably preoccupied about the appointment so Tom turned on the radio for a diversion. They joined a news broadcast in the middle of a report describing the highway death of a drunk driver the night before. State troopers believed the young man fell asleep on his way back from Austin to his barracks in Fort Hood, making it the fifth military personnel road fatality this year. After a loud station identification, the anchorwoman began announcing the current headline. Leading the morning's news was a report on the tropical storm that was making its way through the Gulf of Mexico. The storm had earlier been on course to move northeast along the Atlantic coast but a shift in winds in the upper atmosphere had sent it along the length of Cuba causing extensive damage. It was now expected to move north towards the southeast Texas coast.

"Oh for fuck's sake!" Andy howled.

The anchorwoman continued, "Tropical Storm Albert isn't expected to reach hurricane strength but many residents along the shoreline are boarding up and heading further inland to avoid the brunt of the storm. The memory of Hurricane Ike in 2008 is still fresh on the minds of the communities along the coast and nearly four years later, many homes and businesses still haven't been rebuilt. The National Hurricane Center in Miami are reporting that Tropical Storm Albert is expected to reach the Texas coastline some time Thursday evening. Expect heavy northbound traffic for the next couple of days. In other news -"

Andy turned down the volume and smiled shaking his head, saying, "This is some lucky streak! At this rate I'm more likely to be abducted by aliens or attain Nirvana than have a normal afternoon!" He reached to the back seat for a bottle of water and saw the book Tom brought. He grabbed it and began inspecting the blurbs and book description with fascination. "I can only read so much while in a car without getting carsick. What's this book about?"

"It's not easy to describe. The story follows a family as they're forced to evacuate their town after a chemical spill. There's obviously a lot more to it though... To be honest, I haven't been able to read more than a couple pages at a time. I keep finding myself cycling through the same few words as if they're in some other language."

"Considering all the time you spend reading books, have you ever tried writing one?"

"Once," Tom said smiling bashfully. "It didn't go very well."

"In what way?"

"Well, I started writing it a few years back at the beginning of a summer break. I had two weeks off before the summer classes started so I practically shut myself in my apartment and forced myself to write something that came to me in a dream."

"What's it about?"

"It's a really long story. I don't want to bore you."

Andy smiled and said, "You know, it's a really long drive to Houston..."

"The main character is a young guy named James and the story starts just a few weeks before he finishes his bachelor's degree in Spanish. James falls for a guest lecturer from Argentina named Benjamín and they start seeing each other after spending time together in seminars. Benjamín's an older man in his early-fifties and was a former psychotherapist, but was now filling in for an ill professor at James' university. He had recently written a controversial book on Catholic guilt and the long-term psychological impact it leaves on its gay members."

"Sounds cheery!"

"It's a jolly topic," he said with a smirk. "Anyway, James's postgraduate work required immersion in a Spanish-speaking culture so he decides to go back to Córdoba in Argentina with Benjamín once the term was finished. After living a few weeks in Argentina, James befriends a woman named Susana - an eccentric artist who's a few years older than himself. One day, James invites Susana to his place for dinner, but the second she sees Benjamín, she becomes furious and starts shouting at him. They speak so quickly in the local dialect James can't keep up with the verbal abuse. Suddenly, Susana starts having a panic attack and faints right in front of James and Benjamín after hyperventilating. Benjamín then begins telling James about his tragic past with Susana and why she reacted so wildly towards him.

"The story flashes back to the 1970s when Benjamín was studying in a seminary to become a priest. Benjamín knew he was gay well before he decided to enter the priesthood, but guilt pushed him into believing that a life of celibacy would be easier and more respectable than acting on his urges. He had been living at the seminary for just over a year when he came to realize that the majority of the priests in the area were gay themselves. By day, they stood at the pulpit preaching 'the wages of sin is death,' but when night fell, they were either sleeping with one another or picking up guys in bars. The hypocrisy just became too much for Benjamín; his love for God and fellow man was overshadowed by his disgust for his fellow clergymen. He left the church and moved back with his parents to decide what to do next.

"After months of different jobs and meeting people in a secular environment, Benjamín realized that the one thing he missed most about the priesthood was the chance to talk to people and to help them. After reading a few books on psychotherapy, Benjamín moved to Buenos Aires to study at the university there and then finished his doctorate at Stanford where he stayed a few years as a lecturer until his father died. He moved back to Córdoba to care for his elderly mother and eventually became one of the most respected psychotherapists in the region.

"One of Benjamín's patients was Susana's father, Juan, who suffered from severe anxiety and stress that led to occasional bursts of anger. Before Susana was born, Juan was ordered by the court to undergo a psychological evaluation after he was involved in a brutal fight. He was very guarded with his emotions but after a few sessions and being reassured of patient confidentiality,

Juan finally admitted that he regularly had homosexual urges and didn't know how to deal with them. Juan was more than just a devout Catholic - he was considered a leader of the local church community and regularly organized most of the church's social events with his wife. Thanks to his upbringing, Juan strongly believed that being gay was a horrible, unforgivable sin and any mention of the topic made him uneasy. As they continued their sessions, Benjamín hid his own sexuality from Juan to avoid any unnecessary tension. Benjamín explained to Juan that the repression of his own impulses would only lead to more anxiety, depression, and further violent outbursts. He told Juan that the only way to deal with this side of himself was to come to terms with it as any further denial would only make life harder. Benjamín had such strong empathy for Juan's situation as it was one he knew far too well. As time went on, the sessions grew less frequent but José still regularly kept coming back.

"One evening, as Benjamín met some friends in a gay bar, Juan arrived and was beyond drunk. He had just found out his wife was pregnant with Susana and had been drinking all day in celebration and in secret misery. Seeing Benjamín at the bar confused him, so he stormed out in a fury. Benjamín ran after Juan and eventually calmed him down, but in an act of unhinged desperation, Juan kissed Benjamín. Benjamín was slightly drunk too and didn't fight Juan's advances at first, but he quickly came to his senses. He tried to tell Juan they could no longer see each other in a professional sense, but a yearning came over him that quickly shut him up and had him kissing Juan. They went straight back to Benjamín's house to made love, and Juan silently left shortly afterwards. The next day, Juan called Benjamín's office and explained through tears that he now felt worse than ever before and all he could think about was suicide. Benjamín tried and tried to comfort Juan but by the end of the conversation, Benjamín too was crying as his every word of intended solace was met with impervious dogma. Juan thanked Benjamín for trying to help and hung up. That night he killed himself.

"Benjamín received a letter from Juan a few days later realizing Juan must have mailed it just before committing suicide. In the letter, Juan confessed that he had been harboring serious feelings for Benjamín from their first session. Juan wrote that the love he felt for Benjamín was not real love but was a trick of the Devil. He believed that suicide was a lesser sin than willingly leading a life of homosexuality. What Benjamín didn't know was that Juan left a letter for his wife that admitted his homosexuality. In it he told her he still loved her but knew he couldn't be a good husband or father. Juan's wife didn't know about his fling with Benjamín but she still blamed him for Juan's suicide. She raised Susana on her own and brought her up to believe that Benjamín was responsible for her father's death. The church community publicly condemned Benjamín when they found out he was gay and that he left the priesthood for undisclosed reasons years before. Benjamín soon gave up practicing as a therapist and took a job as a tenured lecturer at Córdoba University.

"The story then returns to the present day, but I never knew how it would end. I figured that if I ever got that far in writing it, the story would tidy itself and take care of the loose ends as it went along. To be perfectly honest, I didn't even get up to writing where James and Susana meet."

"Why not?"

"I was just too self-critical of everything I wrote. After five or six days of berating myself and throwing away page after page, I gave up. Everything I wrote felt like it had no distinctive style and began to remind me of someone else's work, and as I tried to convince myself otherwise, I found myself quoting platitudes and cliches - which only made me feel even more unoriginal! A while back I saw an Alan Bennett play about the composers Auden and

Britten, and one of Auden's lines really wedged itself in my head: 'Style is the sum of one's imperfections.' Last summer, as I ripped a notebook apart in frustration, the line popped into my head again and I thought, *Well - what about substance?* If substance and style are opposites, and if style is the sum of one's imperfections - then substance is surely the sum of one's strengths! But even then I realized that if all my strengths lie in the works of others, then surely my substance couldn't be my own either. What's even worse is that the first thing to come to mind was yet another quote: 'Am I really all the things that are outside of me?' I've kept all my notes for the book just in case I ever feel ready to write, but every summer I rummage through them then talk myself out of trying to write it."

"What was your excuse this year?"

"*You*, dummy! I've been so busy lately I haven't even thought about the book... And stop frowning! I didn't mean that this health stuff has been taking up my time. The last few days I've spent with you - hospital time aside - have been wonderful. I've been enjoying my time with you too much to take up such a boring, solitary pursuit. Is that a good enough excuse for you?"

"Yes it is. Consider yourself absolved."

23

For Tom, the long drive to Houston felt like a blurry montage of incongruous landscapes and eras. Lining the new Pickle Parkway tollroad were frighteningly new towns with shopping centers and home improvement stores nestled strangely yet comfortably into the monotonous gray savanna and rocky hills just outside Austin. On raised highways, Tom and Andy drove over the endless crops and struggling small, Walmart-less towns of the Blackland Prairies, stopping in a town called Bastrop on Highway 71 for coffee and a much needed bathroom break. Headed further east, the brush along the highway was scorched a deep black-brown and the earth was still streaked white with ash from a wildfire last September that destroyed over sixteen hundred homes. The baked grasslands merged into hilly, thickly-wooded forests of pine and elm trees evocative of Canada or Scandinavia - but not Texas. Tom rolled the windows down and slowed as he drove through these alien forests, taking in the unusual sights and peaty smells. The final hours of the drive saw nothing but dreary grasslands whose only attractions were relics of former cotton and corn plantations that had recently become country clubs and gated communities in the floodplains of the Gulf Coast. The concrete overpasses and mammoth billboards of the Houston metropolis came as a welcome change as Tom and Andy drove through the city to their hotel.

They walked in a daze through an eerily quiet lobby to the front desk where a bored, fake-orange-tanned receptionist in her early twenties sat staring at her phone. Her leather swivel chair was turned away from the entrance, leaving her oblivious of her customers. Andy tiptoed to the desk and bellowed, "Hi there! We have a room booked for two nights under the name of Tom Woodbine."

The receptionist shuddered at Andy's booming baritone and spun around to face him with her face quickly turning red.

"Hello sir. If you give me just a moment I'll pull up your details. . . Here they are. Right, so you have a single room for two adults booked for tonight and tomorrow night with us."

"That's correct."

The receptionist looked at Tom holding his bags, then turned to Andy and asked, "Did you want to make that a double room with two beds?"

"No," Andy said. "The one king-sized bed we booked and paid for online should be just fine, thanks."

The receptionist's eyes narrowed as she wordlessly tapped away on her keyboard. The hurried speed and force of her fake nails on the thin plastic keys sounded like small firecrackers.

Tom asked the receptionist, "Is the storm going to affect much around here?"

"There's always a bit of wind damage but Albert got a bit weaker after it hit Cuba, so they don't think it'll be that bad. Plus it's a bit early in the season for a big one. The whole city will probably be pretty quiet until this weekend when it totally passes."

Andy asked, "If that's the case, do you have any rooms high up with a decent view?" After he paid a considerably large surcharge, they went upstairs to their room.

Tom walked in and fell face-first onto the bed. "I can't believe you'd spend that much money on somewhere to sleep." His muffled words were barely audible through the duvet.

"Who said anything about sleeping?"

Tom raised his head a few inches off the bed and glanced over his shoulder. His eyes widened in incredulousness as he saw Andy toplessly gyrating behind him.

"You're ridiculous!"

"Sorry, but hotels always make me horny!" He slowly sashayed towards Tom's prone body. "Besides, we have a little over an hour before I have to be at the hospital. Why not make good use of the time?"

Seeing an unfamiliar wild glow in Andy's eyes, Tom realized he had neither the energy to ward off Andy's advances nor the will to do so. Andy quickly unfastened the rivets on Tom's jeans and yanked them off his legs. Andy breathed heavily as he took off the rest of his and Tom's clothes before climbing atop Tom on the bed, pinning his hands down, and biting him on the collarbone. There was a reckless, almost rude sense of determination in Andy's every move, but Tom was intrigued by his mood and didn't dare resist as Andy assertively moved his limbs about. Tom hid any discomfort as Andy ran his hands through his hair before grabbing it aggressively and pulling Tom's face to his own. And as Andy thrust and thrust, whispering he was ready, Tom winced and pulled Andy further in, embracing him as close as humanly possible. Andy's chest frantically rose and fell as he panted and turned deep red. With his eyes clenched tight, he fell towards Tom, dropping his heavy head on Tom's sweaty chest as he caught his breath. Andy flinched and quivered as he pulled himself away and rolled to the other side of the bed, staring up at the ceiling with a peculiar expression. Though still physically absorbed by his immediate surroundings, there was a distant glint in Andy's eyes and Tom knew full well he was inwardly far, far away.

Tom and Andy both showered quickly and drove straight to the medical center and, almost seconds after they sat down in the unusually chilly admissions waiting room, a young, slender woman with straight black hair tied in a bun walked towards them.

"Mr. Strauss?" the woman asked.

"That's me."

"Hi, I'm Doctor Lesley Hong and I'll be your consultation liaison. If you'll follow me we can go meet the rest of the group."

Tom and Andy stood and followed her purposeful stride down impeccably clean hallways and through several keycard-entry doors. Inside the windowless consultation room were two men in white jackets seated on one side of a long table. At the end of the table was a large, nearly-frameless monitor displaying some of the MRI scans from the day before.

"Please take a seat," Doctor Hong said as she sat between the other doctors. "I know this must look a bit intimidating but we're all here for a reason, Mr. Strauss."

The older of the two men cleared his throat loudly and said, "This isn't a typical consultation. We're in a bit of a peculiar situation regarding your treatment."

"How so?" Andy asked.

"Well, we previously had a craniotomy scheduled for tomorrow morning for a patient with a growth similar to your own. However, the patient has developed a rather severe upper respiratory infection and a high fever, and we just can't operate until she gets better. These sorts of infections can cause complications making surgery much riskier and we don't take chances with such a delicate procedure. As the surgical team is still scheduled to be on-call in theatre, we decided to offer the slot to you. Would you be interested?"

Andy was stunned. After a few silent moments he said, "So let me get this straight - you'd want to operate on me tomorrow morning?"

"Mr. Strauss," the younger male doctor said, "we've all gone over the scans performed yesterday and have already outlined the procedure. I personally watched the scans as they came in through the live feed and I'm convinced that we're dealing with a

176

tumor called a meningioma on your left parietal lobe. Everything about the position of the tumor as well as the shape and density is typical of a meningioma. These are characteristically slow-growing tumors and are usually benign with a good overall prognosis, but we want to take special care as you've shown some rather serious symptoms. Of course, we can't tell for certain if the growth is benign or malignant until a biopsy is performed. Either way, we strongly feel that the best plan of action is to take this window of opportunity and remove the growth without any delay."

"Andy," Dr. Hong said. "I can't stress enough that the speed from detection of a mass to surgical removal is never this immediate, so if you need more time to prepare, we can schedule the operation later next month. I know this is all very spur-of-the-moment and must be overwhelming for you, but it's definitely worth considering."

Andy turned to Tom and looked to him for his approval, his opinion, anything - but all Tom could do was shrug his shoulders.

Andy said, "Fine, let's do it. No point in waiting I guess."

"Brilliant!" Dr. Hong said smiling. "We just need you to fill in some paperwork now, then we'll have a pre-operative briefing to describe in full what the operation entails. After that, our cardiac team is standing by, ready to take a couple more scans to make sure your heart is healthy enough for surgery."

The briefing and pre-operative testing flowed through the following hour and a half in perfect choreography. Andy studiously paid attention as the lights were dimmed and the consultation team went through a brief presentation of the scans on the monitor as well as a computer-animated video of the surgical process. After being taken under by general anesthesia, Andy's head would be placed in a vice-like apparatus to keep it absolutely still throughout the operation. The video showed a graphic of cartoon surgeons making a neat, bloodless C-shaped incision in the scalp, exposing the skull where a tiny burr hole would be drilled. From there, a flap of bone was etched out to reveal the membranes that encase the brain. Once the membranes were incised and folded back, the growth was exposed and removed for biopsy. At the end, a few small screws were put in place to fasten the bone flap to the rest of the skull and thirty-odd staples mended the scalp.

After the video, a nurse took a blood sample from Andy while the team discussed his medical history. Dr. Hong then led Andy and Tom through glaringly-bright corridors to the cardiac department on the third floor. Tom waited in the lobby where he watched daytime court television with dialogue rife of censorial bleeps and tones that seemed to blend into the sounds of the surrounding medical equipment. After Andy's chest x-ray, small spots on his chest and under his arms were shaved where the ECG electrodes were to be connected; he giggled as the cold, plastic pads touched his now bare skin. It was nearly four in the afternoon when the doctors finished their examinations and determined Andy was more than healthy enough for surgery.

Dr. Hong said, "The operation itself should take at least six hours, but may go on a bit longer. We ask that you don't eat or drink anything after around seven o'clock tonight as anything in your stomach could come right back up when you're under anesthesia. Have a light meal tonight, no alcohol, and try to get a good night's sleep as we'll be starting bright and early in the morning. It's important that we get you in one of the neuro-ICU recovery rooms on the opposite side of the building well before the storm hits so where there won't be any direct gusts. Even if there was a full-force hurricane, you'd still be safe and sound there. Once you're fully lucid after the operation, we'll go over a post-surgery plan, but until then please don't hesitate to contact us if you have any more questions."

"Thanks," Andy said, "I think you covered everything and more."

Dr. Hong turned to Tom, put her hand on his shoulder, and insistently looked him in the eyes. "I can tell that he's a handful, but make sure he eats a nice, healthy meal tonight and gets to bed early. He needs to be here no later than seven in the morning, but the earlier you get here, the better. The surgeons like an early start."

"I'll do what I can."

24

Tom and Andy ate in a small candlelit French bistro near the hotel in Rice Village. Andy ordered a small bowl of crab bisque and a beetroot salad with goat's cheese while Tom had a confit leg of duck and *tarte tatin* at Andy's insistence. After eating, Andy leaned back in his chair with his head resting on the side of a large walnut wine rack; its contents presumably worth more than Tom and Andy's combined personal worth.

"Just before I moved to Belton, I ran into an old lawyer friend from a rival firm. Years before, back when I was still practicing, we used to meet up in motels to sleep with each other. We'd joke that when we weren't at each others' throats in court, we liked to spend our spare time tending to other parts our our bodies - but there was something about our competitive work relationship that made these encounters that much more interesting. Anyway, his wife and kids were out of town and he invited me over for the night - something we never did. After a really intense *session,* we had a few glasses of scotch and watched the news in his living room. It was the night the governor announced he was pulling out of the Republican primary race and I remember getting really fired up, saying something like, 'His pulling out of the race is the best thing to happen to American politics this century! But you know, I wouldn't be surprised if that bastard came back here to announce Texas' independence from the US, then build great big electrified fences along the border, dotted with watchtowers armed by pro-lifers.'"

Tom tried to hide his smile as a few shocked diners nearby listened in.

"I just went on and on about nothing and my friend kept

quiet and let me rant until I was practically out of breath. When I finally stopped he crossed his arms and looked down his nose at me saying, 'You know, I've been a Republican all my life and I donated a couple grand to his campaign last year. Plus, he's a Texas boy - it's like supporting the home team.'"

Andy held his palms up in exasperation. "I mean - I just didn't get it! This was coming from a guy I slept with only moments before! I was just out of the closet by then and he was still married with kids, but he knew exactly what the Governor's policies were regarding homosexuality. Hell, the entire country knew what his policies were because they were the fucking cornerstone of his campaign! And when someone's that gay-obsessed, you know there's always an underlying issue. Anyway, this friend of mine went on and on about how gay people didn't need the same recognition as the rest of the public, that we've always existed on the fringe of society. Equality in marriage, child custody, employment protection, benefits, whatever - all of it was a joke to him. So I went online on my phone and looked up the website of the Texas Republican Party to show the guy their official platform stance on homosexuality - particularly the part that said 'it tears at the fabric of society, contributes to the breakdown of the family unit, and leads to the spread of dangerous, communicable diseases'. He just shrugged and said, 'So what - people have said that stuff for generations and it's not going to change any time soon.' I was just so frustrated, I stormed out of his house and never talked to him again."

Andy sipped his mineral water and glanced at a middle-aged woman at the adjacent table who'd been noticeably eavesdropping. She wore a navy suit with a bold white lapel and a large yellow enamel rose brooch. As she quickly turned away to avoid eye contact with him, she loudly knocked a fork to the floor.

Andy turned back to Tom and said, "It just upsets me that

there are so many people like him that just latch onto some pattern or ideology just because their parents did, because their parents did, and on and on..."

"So what - that's life. It's been like that for generations and it's not going to change any time soon," Tom said with a smirk.

"Well, it fucking should!"

Tom watched the lady in navy nudge her husband then angrily whisper something into his ear. Eager to avoid any confrontation, Tom called the waiter over and asked for the bill. As they left, Andy stuck his tongue out at the woman and laughed as she grimaced.

Once outside, Tom smirked and said, "That poor woman..."

"She didn't know who she was dealing with," Andy said.

"I bet you've permanently put her off gay people. She'll think we're all heathens like yourself."

"Aren't we though?"

"Speak for yourself!"

"Well, speaking for myself, I can honestly say I couldn't give a shit what she may or may not think. And furthermore, I've never left that restaurant still feeling hungry, which is in itself a travesty. Damn this operation keeping me from gorging myself on rich foods! ... How was your duck?"

"Stunning, but anything cooked in that amount of fat, butter, and salt is going to be."

"And the tart?"

"Same rules apply."

"We should go there again once this is all over," Andy said flicking his hair.

"Count me in."

Back in the hotel room, Tom and Andy arranged two armchairs near the window to watch the cloudless sky as the sun slowly set. They sat in silence peering out towards the invisible sea for any sign of an approaching storm, but all that hung in the sky were streaky vapor trails glowing pink and orange above the sticky Houston haze. Though physically worn down, Andy's mind anxiously raced on. Tom massaged Andy's feet, shoulders, back - anything to try to relax him. Andy's stomach growled in emphatic protest against the pre-surgery fasting. Shuffling in his seat, he reached into his pocket for his phone.

He said, "I should probably tell my dad."

Tom heard a few muffled rings before a low, succinct voicemail greeting.

"Hi Dad, it's Andy. ... There's really no other way to say this: I'm having an operation tomorrow morning at the medical center. I'll probably be in Houston for a little while afterwards and thought you should know. Anyway, you've got my number. I hope you're well. Bye."

Andy tossed his phone onto the bed and slumped into his chair.

Tom asked, "Is there anyone else you want to call?"

"Like who - my ex-wife? Some of the guys I used to sleep with? Or maybe I could call my family who haven't spoken to me since I came out! Like they'd even give a damn!"

"... I'm only trying to help."

Andy shamefully threw his head back and said, "Sorry, I know you were. I'm on edge and hungry - never a good combination for me. Could you just ignore anything I say for the rest of the evening?"

"Consider it done."

25

The startling, unfamiliar ring of the hotel phone on the nightstand shook Tom awake. He gracelessly slung his limp hand at the phone and reeled it back in.

"Hello?"

A young man answered with a chirpy liveliness. "Good morning sir! This is the front desk with your five-forty-five wake-up call! Just so you know, breakfast services start at six. Will you be dining with us this morning?"

Tom was shell-shocked. "... I honestly have no idea. I'll let you know later, thank you."

"Thank *you* sir! Have a nice day!"

Tom returned the phone to its base and drowsily turned over to find himself alone in bed. Looking across the room, he saw a thin shred of foggy light glowing under the bathroom door. The hiss of the running shower and the peculiar smell of pre-surgical detergent roused Tom out of bed to his feet. He slipped into his white hotel robe and walked to a gap in the drawn curtains to peer out at the early morning stars gently shining through the clear, dark sky.

The rest of the morning seemed to pass Tom by in a hazy rush. After showering, he and Andy skipped breakfast and headed straight to the hospital, walking the quiet streets as the sun rose. Through cool, the morning air was viscously humid and seemed to cake over the dew of the night. At admissions, Andy was greeted with a stack of paperwork to sign before he was taken to a small room where he was given an identification bracelet and a surgical gown. As Tom waited in the lobby, staring at an aquarium, he could feel his entire body shaking and wasn't sure if it was the lack of deep sleep, the hunger from skipping breakfast, or sheer stress that was making him tremble.

He thought, *All I need to do is stand here and do my best to be encouraging and stable, nothing else - but I can't even do that.*

As the nurses shaved a large patch on Andy's scalp and prepared a vein on the back of his hand for an IV catheter, Andy smiled calmly at Tom. He looked into Tom's eyes and grabbed Tom's arm pulling him near.

"Tom, I love you."

Tom's eyes flooded with tears. "I love you too."

"I wanted to tell you days ago, but I was afraid. But now that I'm laying here, I'm afraid not to. I just can't go in there without letting you know I love you." Andy saw Tom's hand trembling as it held the cream plastic bed rail and he reached over and squeezed it tightly. "I know you're scared, but I'll be fine."

Andy looked composed, as ready as he ever could be, as he was wheeled to the operating room. As they arrived, Dr. Hong stepped through the doors and said, "It's time to go in, Mr. Strauss."

Tom leaned in and kissed Andy on his new bald spot, prompting a scowling nurse to swoop in and scrub it with a sanitary wipe.

"I'll be here when you get out," Tom said.

"Me too."

"I love you."

"I love you too."

Andy was rolled out of sight, smiling all the way.

The television in the surgical waiting room blared the morning news from a local station.

"The storm has weakened significantly since passing over Cuba, but meteorologists are still expecting substantial property damage. Residents along the coast should be prepared for very high winds and possible flooding."

The presenter paused as footage of the battered Cuban beaches changed to photographs of several young men killed by an explosive overseas.

"A series of bombs set off by insurgents yesterday in Afghanistan has killed 7 NATO soldiers, five of which were American. The families of the slain soldiers have been notified. Their deaths take the total of American personnel killed since the _"

Tom switched off the television and slumped into his seat. A dying fluorescent bulb flickered over his head.

"Hey asshole - I was watching that!"

A tall man across the room stood from his chair with clenched fists and baggy eyes. It was obvious he had been waiting for quite some time.

Tom thought, *I'll lose my mind if I wait here.* He switched the television back on and walked out of the room, ignoring the man's angry glare. The crisp morning breeze hit Tom in the face as he walked out of the medical center doors towards Herrmann Park and the Houston Zoo. The disparate clamoring choruses of eager customers waiting outside the zoo and the noisy residents within did little to help Tom compose himself. A group of children began to mimic the cries of the chimpanzees near the gate and in seconds the aping spread through the lines and echoed throughout the park. Tom felt a buzz in his pocket and faintly heard the ringtone of his phone buried under the cacophony around him. A picture of his mother glowed on the phone's screen.

"Hello?"

"Tom why didn't you tell me you were in Houston? You know we're only half an hour away!"

"Hi Mom."

"Your sister told us about Andy - how's he doing?"

"Well, he's actually in surgery right now; the specialists had an opening in their schedule and he took it."

Anne gasped. "Oh my God!"

"They're removing what they think is a meningioma, some sort of tumor on his brain."

"We're coming over! Where are you?"

"Mom, you really don't have to."

"We're going to be driving that way this afternoon anyway. We're spending the weekend at your sister's to get away from the storm. I'm sure your father would love to see you too. Where are you staying?"

"Near the medical centre on Fannin Street."

"We'll be there in a couple hours when we finish packing and we'll take you out for lunch, okay honey? Bye!" And she hung up.

Just like Sam - when she's done talking to you, she's done talking to you.

After a convoluted series of navigational text messages, Tom met his parents in the busy lobby of a family cafeteria-style restaurant near his hotel. Tom's father Jim smiled widely on seeing his son as he held the door open for Anne. She entered the lobby wearing a bright pink sundress and her high-heels clicked loudly as she jogged up to hug her son.

"Mom, you look great!"

"Thanks baby. I don't get to see you often enough so I thought I'd make an effort." She let go of Tom and flicked her bangs away from her forehead. "Sorry we're a little late. Your father got his shirt dirty and needed to change."

Jim threw his heavy arms around Tom and said, "Some of the window shutters wouldn't lock so I had to cinch them shut with cable ties."

He stepped back and looked into his son's tired eyes.

"Boy, you look like hell."

With plastic trays in hand, the Woodbines snaked through the cafeteria, then sat in a white vinyl booth with steamy, fried comfort food piled high on their plates. Sweaty translucent red plastic cups full of iced tea and various condiments dotted the table. At Anne's request, Jim took a napkin from the chrome dispenser near the wall and wore it like a bib.

Anne asked, "So how is Andy holding up?"

"I guess he's doing okay. He's been a bit on-edge but that's more than understandable. I don't really have a frame of reference for this sort of thing."

"Mm-hmm. And what about you? This all must be pretty stressful."

"Sure it is, but I honestly don't feel like I can complain. I'm not the one in the life-threatening situation. I feel like all I can do is be there for him, you know?"

Tom looked at them both as they nodded. He thought, *Now's as good a time as any.*

"Mom, Dad... Andy's my boyfriend."

Anne brought a napkin to cover her mouth and said, "We know, honey."

"You know?"

She laughed and said, "Well, your soon-to-be brother-in-law Tom told me yesterday when I called to make arrangements for this weekend. Tom really thinks highly of Andy. He sends his love, by the way. Plus, I could tell there was some chemistry between you two when I met him on Saturday. You know, it's about damn time you've met someone!"

Tom was shocked. "How long have you known I was gay?"

"Sam spilled the beans years ago - only a few days after you told her. I can't remember why, but she and I were on the phone arguing and she blurted out 'Tom's gay!' - as if it would give her some sort of leverage in the conversation. She went on and on about how wrong and sinful she thought it was, and I remember feeling totally dumbstruck by her blind contempt. I thought 'This hateful woman isn't my daughter. This isn't the little girl I brought up.' After that argument, she and I didn't speak to each other for quite a while."

"I had no idea."

"That's because I didn't want you to know. You were in the last couple months of your degree in Austin and I didn't want to give you anything else to stress about. Besides, Sam and I reconciled a few weeks later when she called to announce her first engagement. I tried talking about you again, but you know how stubborn she is. I decided it was pointless to try and reason with her. At times I have to remind myself that Sam's one of those Christians who talks the way she does because she thinks she's supposed to - especially when she knows there's an audience. But that's just her way and there's no telling her otherwise. Thankfully she's calmed down quite a bit since Brandon and Shelley came along."

Tom shook his head in disbelief. "So if you knew for so long, why didn't either of you say anything?"

"Tom, honey, what could we have said? Your father and I love and respect you. We never wanted to push you into coming out or doing anything against your will. We figured you would tell us if and when you wanted us to know."

Jim measuredly said, "All we want is for you to be happy. Nothing can change that."

"And Tom, when Andy gets better I expect you both to come visit us. A bit of sea air would be good for him. Now eat up

189

before your food goes cold!"

Over coffee and pie, Anne spoke in length about some of the wedding plans she and Sam had been arranging while Tom and Jim exchanged glances of serene obliviousness. Anne noticed a few of their occasional smirks but said nothing; her contentment was obvious. By one-thirty, the Woodbines stood in the restaurant parking lot exchanging hugs.

"Sorry we've got to dash off, but rush-hour traffic on top of everyone evacuating the coast is going to make getting to Sam's by dinnertime damn near impossible."

"It's okay Mom. It was good to see you both."

"We can drop you off at the hospital or your hotel if you'd like."

"Thanks but I'd rather walk off some of this food," Tom said, holding his belly. "I love you guys, you know."

"We love you too," they replied in unison.

Like a gleeful child, Tom waved to his parents as they drove away from the restaurant. The elation of finally living an open life had washed over him, and as he walked back towards the hospital, not even the heavy, gravy-laden food sloshing in his belly nor the afternoon heat could shake his spirit.

After seven and a half hours of surgery, Tom stood at the side of Andy's bed as he slowly regained consciousness in the recovery room. Tom held Andy's left hand and felt Andy's fingers as they slowly wriggled and weaved into his own with each conscious stir. Almost all of Andy's head was wrapped in a helmet of bandages with only his swollen face . A couple of plastic tubes ran from a small plastic box at the top of his head that monitored and regulated the pressure inside his skull. On a clipboard next to Andy's bed, Tom read off a checklist of the operative procedures - BrainLAB neuronavigation, parietal craniotomy, subparietal decompression, tumor removal, duraplasty, ICP monitor... It could have read anything and Tom would have still been just as relieved.

"Everything went as we expected," Dr. Hong said. "The surgeons completely removed the meningioma without any complications and the biopsy showed the tumor to be benign. There's still about a one-in-five chance of recurrence so we'll need him back in over the next few months for more scans. You know, Andy was very lucky that we could move so quickly."

"Tom?" Andy mumbled. "Are you okay?"

"Me? Of course I'm okay! I'm not the one who just came out of surgery!"

"Good, good." Andy smiled and gently squeezed Tom's hand.

Constantly drifting off to sleep, Andy didn't speak much for the rest of the night. His dedicated nurse was required to wake him up every hour and have him complete several simple neurological tests and Andy scowled at her each time she came.

Just before nine o'clock, the nurse came over and said, "Sir, just so you know, visiting hours will be over soon. You're welcome to stay the night here, but you won't be able to leave this ward. We'll continue to wake him up every hour, so if you plan on sleeping tonight, I'd recommend staying somewhere else. He's not going anywhere."

"You're right. I'll come back in the morning." Hearing this, Andy awoke on his own and held his arms out to Tom like a baby wanting to be picked up. Tom leaned in, carefully avoiding the many hoses and cables dangling from Andy's arms and neck, and gently hugged him, kissing him on the nose.

"Love you Andy."

He slurred, "Love you too."

Outside, the wind howled as it rushed between the tall towers of the medical center. Misty rain was whipped into Tom's face as he jogged back to the hotel, and as the weather progressively worsened, Tom began to sprint, laughing as he imagined what he'd have to encounter on tomorrow morning's hospital visit. Tom felt his phone vibrating in his pocket as he ran, but he didn't dare expose it to the elements. He walked through the main doors straight to the front desk and ordered a sandwich, salad, and a large glass of wine from room service. In the elevator, he checked his phone and saw that Susan had left a voicemail:

'Hi Mr. Woodbine! I know you said to call you Tom, but it's still too weird for me. Anyway, I saw on the news that the tropical storm was starting to hit the coast and I wanted to call and see how you two were. Dad's taking me and Robby to see a movie in a few minutes so I won't be able to talk later, but call me tomorrow afternoon if you can. I've booked a campus visit in Temple the morning to check out the nursing department. Anyway, give Andy a kiss for me! Bye!'

The hotel's incessant air-conditioning on Tom's wet skin made him shiver all the way up to the nineteenth floor. As soon as he entered his room, he stripped his damp clothes off and took a quick shower before room service could bring up his meal. With his feet propped up on the table, Tom ate his meal on the sofa in his robe while watching a live weather broadcast on the television, complete with the obligatory meteorologist in a rain slicker stood on the pier as horizontal rain and waves lashed around him. As the tortured weatherman tried to shout over the shrieking gales, Tom opened an email from his mother and waited for the attached image to slowly download and open on his phone's screen. Tom turned his phone sideways and double-tapped the screen to enlarge the image, and as he held it up to his face, his eyes began to fill with tears. In the picture, Jim, Anne, and Sam faced the camera with Brandon and Shelley on their knees holding two separate pieces of paper that said 'Get Well' and 'Soon Andy!'. The email itself read: 'Lots of love from all of us back home - stay dry!'

Tom spent the rest of the night reading at the window with the curtains fully open. Once the initial wind and rain hit, there was really nothing else for Tom to see but a constant wall of grey, undulating mist.

He laughed and thought, *All that extra money for a better view, just to watch a bit of rain.*

With wine in his hand and the soft audial wash of the rain on the reinforced glass window, Tom finished reading his book by eleven. He stood and stretched as he finished the last sentence then rested his forehead against the window, looking down at the street and watching the illuminated wisps of the storm as they snaked through the empty streets. Tom pulled away to drink the last drops of wine from his glass, then walked to the desk on the far side of the room. As he set the wineglass down, he noticed the hotel notepad was full of what he immediately recognized as Andy's handwriting. As Tom read, he wildly laughed and cried, holding the notepad at arm's length to keep his tears from falling on the pages. Once finished, Tom laid down on the bed, exhausted and overcome with rapturous emotion. Every part of his life had come together and he knew that at this moment, he felt more alive, more connected to life itself than he had ever felt before.

26

'It's 3:03 AM on Thursday, May 30th and Tom is in bed behind me asleep with one leg sticking out from the sheets. Before he finally nodded off he suggested I should keep a journal detailing this whole surgery/recovery experience to help me make sense of everything. I'm sure it really is a good idea, but I bet a big part of him mentioned it just to shut me up. I know he'd deny it, but by now he's got to be sick of hearing me bitch and moan about everything.

I don't really know where to start with this journal thing so I guess I'll start at the beginning of the hospital visits:

Waking up in the hospital on Tuesday really fucked me up. I know it's impossible to be prepared for a health scare like this, but facing this has really stirred some thoughts and views I haven't dealt with in a very long time. When I was surrounded by the loud hum in the MRI machine, there was nothing to do but obsess on whatever thought popped up - and unsurprisingly it was hard to think of anything else aside from the tumor. At first, I thought it was kinda funny that I could grow something within myself - intentionally or not - that could affect me in such a strange way. I guess it was inevitable that I eventually started thinking about the possibility of this <u>thing</u> killing me. I found myself questioning the paths I've taken and the decisions I've made throughout my life, and I couldn't tell if this was from some deeply buried Catholic guilt over something from my past or a fleeting sense of some vague, unfulfilled aspiration I've yet to understand. It was like my thoughts darted around in a panic trying to decipher what's essentially indecipherable and, since the scan, I've felt a bit detached from reality as if none of this is actually happening.

When Tom and I left my house for Houston, I mentally prepared myself for never coming back. I've never been very materialistic but I tried to rouse some bullshit sentimental longing for my new house, but I couldn't feel anything for it or any of the things inside. Then, when we actually got to Houston and talked to the doctors, everything seemed to spiral out of my control and I started feeling even more despondent. I know I'm lucky to get the chance to sort out this tumor - but I sure as hell don't feel very lucky right now.

I don't really know why I'm writing this, or even to whom I'm writing. If this is a journal and the operation is a full success, I know I won't read it again. I'll probably fold these sheets up and put them in a book or folder somewhere only to come across them years later. ~~If it's not a success and something happens to me~~

Ignore that. I want to go into this positively. Any more self-reflection at 3 AM on an empty stomach is only going to turn into unhealthy obsession.

Tom has been my rock throughout this whole mess. I know we only met a few days ago but I feel like he knows me better than anyone else ever has. Sitting here just a few feet away from him, watching him sleep so peacefully, I keep picturing all the things I want to do with him... and not just the the big, obvious things like living together or going on vacation. I want to do all the silly little things you take for granted like cooking a meal together, or going out to see a film, or falling asleep on his shoulder. A huge part of me wants to wake him up and tell him I love him, but I don't want to overwhelm him and scare him off. He's all I have now - and I'm okay with that. There's nobody else I'd rather be with. I really do love him.

When I come out of this, I'm going right back to that

Japanese place with Tom. I'm so fucking hungry right now and all I can think about are those goddamn plates of sushi.

I can't concentrate. I'm going to bed.'

After writing, Andy spent the rest of his sleepless morning in bed holding his body close to Tom's, deeply breathing in Tom's sweet scent and gently running his fingers through Tom's hair, trying not to wake him. Later, as he lay in his gurney in the operating room, Andy found himself surrounded by the sights and sounds of far more machines, braces, cables, screens, and people than he assumed necessary. The brave face he put on for Tom quickly faded. The mechanical beeps of the apparatuses crescendoed as the nurses connected his IV cannulas and sensors to various bags and devices. Andy found himself torn equally between a fear for his life and a sensation of contentment and love - each fueling the other. Feeling powerless, he wept.

A doctor stands over Andy and tells him to count backwards from **ten** as he slowly empties a syringe into one of the many clear plastic tubes. Andy wipes his sweaty palms on his thin blue surgical gown. **Nine.** He feels his breaths get deeper and deeper. A masked nurse puts her hand on Andy's collarbone, gently massaging it. **Eight.** The bright surgical light positioned over Andy's head makes him squint and a couple of stray tears slowly trickle down his temples to his ears. **Seven.** Andy feels his eyelids droop as the lights and sounds around him blur. He imagines sleeping next to Tom. **Six.**

27

In the great room of an ancient stately home, a man with a short silver beard stands in front of Andy; his face virtually blends into the array of countless gold-framed portraits lining the dark walnut panel walls. Andy hears the footsteps of many people echoing off the marble floors; the low murmur of their hushed words hum throughout the house. The man with the silver beard takes Andy by the arm and forcefully ushers him into the kitchen. As they enter the room through a massive doorway. Andy sees Tom being rushed past in the opposite direction by a doppelgänger of the man with the silver beard. Tom's face looks devoid of any emotion or concern. Seated in an ornate throne at the head of a long oval table is an elegantly dressed middle-aged woman. Her flowing deep black hair cascades down past several strands of pearls adorning her slender neck to the shoulder-straps of her glossy blue silk ballroom gown. The man with the silver beard escorts Andy to a high-backed chair near the woman and motions for him to sit down.

"What's happening?" Andy asks.

The man with the silver beard lowers his head to the woman and slowly recedes from the room, never once turning his back to the woman.

Without looking at Andy, the woman slowly raises her chin and says, "It would be best for you not to think about what's happening here." The lean muscles in her neck gently dance as she talks.

Andy slams his fists against the table and yells, "Who are those men?!"

The warm, sooty odor of a campfire swiftly fills the air. The woman turns to Andy and gracefully takes his hand. Andy is immediately transfixed by the extravagant antique jewelry covering her long, willowy fingers. She says, "You don't need to know."

"What is that supposed to mean? Where are we?"

The woman gently strokes Andy's face; the touch of her cool gold rings on his cheek makes him flinch. "Where we are doesn't matter. As long as you keep calm, you'll be fine. This is all I'm allowed to tell you. You must trust me."

She clears her throat to get Andy's attention and stares deep into his eyes. Andy feels overcome with the sense of urgency. The woman takes Andy's hands, squeezes them, and says, "This is how it must happen."

Her eyes roll back in her head as she flings herself back into her throne. She begins to convulse and a pulsating sound washes out of her into Andy's hands, spreading throughout the rest of his body like a sustained electric shock. Tears stream down Andy's face as he grimaces and twists, gnashing his teeth in torment as the surge reaches his head where it reverberates and wildly self-oscillates into a wall of noise. The woman comes to, quickly stands, and runs to put her delicate arms around Andy from behind, holding him tightly to her fragile body. Her long black hair has fallen across her face and Andy can hear her pearls loudly rattle as he slams into her with each of his torturous jerks. Now fearing for the safety of them both, Andy sweats and strains as he fights the tremors with every ounce of his being, and after a few agonizing deep breaths, Andy loses consciousness and the sharp tone in his head slowly fades into absolute silence.

Andy wakes up face-down on the table; his eyes feel fatigued and swollen from sleep. He faintly sees the woman in his blurry periphery and asks, "How long was I out?" but the woman merely glances at him without a reply. Sitting poised with her arms crossed, now in elbow-length white gloves, she looks as immaculate as when Andy was escorted into the room.

Andy thought, *Did any of that even happen?*

He looks down at the table and traces the grain of the wood with his fingers. The wood is dry and worn with crunchy, fractured flecks of an old honey-colored varnish barely clinging to the surface. Andy picks up a flake of the varnish and grinds it between his fingers until it turns to a fine yellow powder. As he sprinkles the powder over the table to free it from his fingers, it floats upwards to the ceiling and begins to flicker with light like thousands of tiny candles. The woman stands from her throne at the sound of a ringing digital chime tone. Suddenly, Andy's ears feel clogged as all sound is sucked from the room. A wave of familiar serenity washes over him as he stops and looks at his hands to find them much, much older and covered in unfamiliar purple blotches. He silently laughs as he pinches and plays with the thin skin on the back of his hands. Another pair of hands appears from the sides and clasps Andy's, holding them tightly. Though they too are old and knobbly, Andy knows these strong hands. As their worn fingers weave together, a bright coral-colored light floods the room and Andy's eyes fill with tears as he senses Tom's warm, kind touch.

Acknowledgements

I am truly grateful to the brave souls who tolerated me through the few months it took to write this. I can only imagine the headaches and dull emotional trauma I must have incurred on you. I am especially appreciative to Sarah Ramsden for allowing me to reference her informative yet infinitely warm blog *Me, Myself, & Meningioma* (memyselfmeningioma.wordpress.com) - a personal chronicle of her dealings with an olfactory groove meningioma 'from diagnosis through recovery'. I am also grateful to Francis Egly for allowing me to visit and observe her classroom in December 2011. Special thanks to Christina Croft, Max Price, Paul Everitt, and Ben Styles for reading this novel at an early stage and providing their invaluable comments and support. Thank you to my mother, father, brother, and extended family back in Texas for continually motivating me to push on with this project. Most of all, thank you to my partner, Dominic Bull, for enthusiastically reading several stages of draft and never holding back a word when he thought something needed changing. Without you, Dom, I'd be lost.

Printed in Poland
by Amazon Fulfillment
Poland Sp. z o.o., Wrocław